Stupid Hearts

An Erotic Novella
Kristen Hope Mazzola

Stupid Hearts

Published: Kristen Hope Mazzola 2015:

Cover Design: Kristen Hope Mazzola
Formatting by: Kristen Hope Mazzola

Editing by:
C. Marie editingbycmarie@gmail.com

DEDICATION:

To everyone who dares to fall in love, fast or slow, with their whole heart.

CHAPTER 1.

Well, crap.

Got home from a long ass shoot in Virginia Beach at the ass crack of dawn after a terrible flight full of turbulence and a screaming baby. Made sure Dozer was all settled in, filled up his food and water bowls, fluffed his oversized bed in the living room, and made sure he was happily gnawing on a gigantic rawhide. Finally took a deep breath as I slipped off my favorite dark brown and black ostrich boots.

I slunk into my closet-sized bathroom and started running the water. It looked like Pepto-Bismol had puked all over the damn thing. From the tiles to the bathtub and even the toilet, it was saturated in the awful pink color. The old pipes complained loudly until steaming hot water bellowed from the faucet.

I stripped off my typical black loose fitting V-neck and skintight black skinny jeans, then stood staring at my tired eyes in the mirror. The curls had fallen out of my hair a while ago and the makeup I'd applied at four in the morning was smudged and faded. I looked like a freaking train wreck standing like a Looney Tune in my underwear. I peeled off my black lace bra and matching thong and sank into a much needed scalding hot bath to relax.

After toweling off, throwing my long dark brown locks into a messy dripping bun, and slipping into my pajamas at eleven o'clock in the morning, the only thing left to do was unpack my carry-on bag.

By far my least favorite part of the whole traveling for work thing was living out of a suitcase. Oh, and the never ending laundry once I finally got home.

It continued to be a typical Monday morning until I started to go through the zipped pocket of my suitcase where I normally stowed all of my intimates, including my pink bullet vibrator. What the hell did I find?

Nothing.

All of my favorite thongs were gone. All of my beautiful lace bras that matched those thongs were gone. Devastation set in fast when I realized my favorite vibrator—the one that had been on the road with me for the past three years—was gone.

Well crap!

After three hours of no luck with complaining about the travesty of my stolen intimates to anyone that picked up the phone, I slumped onto the couch to stew in a pissed off channel surfing escapade and mourn the loss of my battery powered o-maker.

My phone buzzed on the light wooden coffee table, next to where my socked feet were resting. The screen displayed an unknown eight-hundred number.

I answered, "This is Jolene."

An automated voice came on the line. "Hello. It has come to our attention that you were dissatisfied with our customer service regarding luggage handling. Please hold for a customer service operator."

Fester.

Fester.

Fester.

At that point my blood was boiling and I was ready to bite the head off of this customer service operator.

"Hello. This is Maureen. It appears that you placed a complaint call earlier today. Please confirm your name for me."

"Jolene Abbott."

"Thank you, Ms. Abbott. How are you doing today?"

She seemed so sweet. Her vanilla-coated voice cooed into the phone, but I didn't give a rat's ass. I seethed, "You want to know how the hell I am doing? I get home from my business trip to find that some pervert that works for y'all in baggage handling gets off on stealing women's intimates. Now I am left with none of my nice underwear or my favorite vibrator! Yes, I did just say vibrator! And y'all won't do a damn thing because there isn't a record of anyone searching my bag. Of course the perv didn't leave a damn record of his sick little game and of course y'all won't help me. So I'm sorry, Maureen. I know you're just doing your job, but I am freaking pissed and y'all either need to reimburse me for the personal property that was stolen from me or just leave me the heck alone."

There was a brief pause.

Maybe I'd been too harsh?

Finally her sweet voice came back on the line, a little softer this time. "I'm very sorry to hear that ma'am. I can transfer you to my supervisor. He might be able to help you."

"Fuck this." Click.

I threw on a Lynyrd Skynyrd shirt and a pair of faded gray skinny jeans, slid my socked feet back into my boots, and applied a light layer of eyeliner and mascara to avoid looking completely dead.

Tossing my phone into my purse, I gave Dozer a few kisses on his egg-shaped head. "Be back in a bit, bud." His whip-like tail thumped against the plush bed as I walked to the door. Right as I pulled my bag's strap over my shoulder and opened the front door, he closed his eyes.

Typical.

I shrugged and started to make my way down the ten flights of stairs.

Time to go shopping.

A successful Victoria's Secret trip was not all that I had planned for this shopping excursion. I hailed a cab, hopped in, and without giving it a second thought, instructed the cabby to take me to "Seventh Avenue South and Charles Street, please."

"Alright." He grinned at me in the rearview mirror, eying my pink striped bag and showing off his lack of teeth along with the ones he did have left, which were stained piss yellow and looked to be hanging on by a thread.

Gross.

I slid out of the cab at the end of the block and made my way to The Pleasure Chest. The faded red brick exterior and the light gray awning did not do the sexual wonderland justice.

A bell chimed overhead as I was greeted by a rather large middle-aged woman. She was covered in tattoos and leaning on the front counter, looking bored out of her skull.

"How can I help please you today?"

The greeting made me giggle. "I have come because of a travesty."

She gasped and came around the counter to help comfort me in my devastated state. "What happened?" She softly put her pudgy hand—which was decorated with a brightly colored cupcake tattoo—onto my shoulder.

"My Iconic Bullet was stolen!"

The woman gasped again, louder this time, and threw

her cupcake hand to her chest. "Well let's find you a new pocket-sized boyfriend."

I grinned and followed her to the back wall, past the sexy roleplaying costumes, anal plugs, and strap-ons.

"Now, you might like something like this." She held up a white ball that looked like it was wearing a weird pink crown.

Nope!

"That is interesting," I faked, not wanting to hurt her feelings. "What's it called?"

"This one is the Vibratex Girls Princessa. My girlfriend loves to roll it around on my clit while I'm climaxing."

Way too much information.

I grabbed a LoveLife Discover from the wall and read its specs: *Discover the pleasure of this versatile mini vibe! Made of silicone and USB rechargeable, this sweet little vibrator has seven delicious settings and is perfect for travel or for a not-so-quiet night in.*

Pink. Simple. *My kind of thing.*

"I think this is the one."

She nodded and within a few minutes I was curbside, trying to hail another taxi to take me home. A cab finally pulled up and right as I was going for the door handle, another hand got there first.

"Excuse me, this is *my* cab," I barked, turning to the owner of the rude hand.

I was greeted by stunning ice blue eyes, a strong stubble-covered jawline, and a huge toothy grin.

"Sorry." His voice was deep and velvety, matching his five thousand dollar suit well. He started to back away from the cab and I panicked. I needed to see more of those eyes so I blurted out, "We could share? I'm heading to the Upper East Side."

He nodded. "So am I."

We hopped in and I gave the directions to my overpriced Fifth and Seventy-sixth,apartment that overlooked Central Park.

My cabmate chuckled.

"Was something I said funny to you, sir?" I drawled at him in the most southern belle voice I could muster.

"It's not every day that a bohemian looking southerner lives in that area of town."

"Excuse me?"

"Forgive me, but you don't *look* like you'd live there." His finger twirled around my outfit. I saw red.

Who the hell does he think he is?

The cab stopped in front of my building and I got out, slamming the door shut without so much as a backward glance at the asshat I'd had the misfortune of sharing a cab with. Beautiful or not, an asshat is an asshat, and I was not going to take shit from someone like that.

"Miss?"

I heard his velvet-coated voice call from the parked cab and the door shut behind him.

"What?" An exasperated tone escaped me as I turned to meet his stunning eyes and a cruel smile raking across his lips.

"You left this in the cab."

To my horror, he was holding my new toy in his hand.

All kinds of red prickled my face as I took my vibrator from him. "Thanks," I choked, gulping the last bit of saliva out of my drying mouth.

"Want to have drinks later?"

I was rather taken aback by his question. "What?"

"I'm only in town a few nights a month and I leave in the morning. I'm free after my next meeting and would love to have some company at the hotel lounge instead of drinking by myself."

He handed me a business card that read "Seth Roberts, CFO" with an address scribbled on the back. "That's where I am staying. I'll be in the lobby around eight. See you there if you'd like."

He got back in the cab while I stood like an idiot, grasping his card in one hand, my vibrator and lingerie bag in the other.

What a freaking weird day!

CHAPTER 2.

I am so out of place!

That's all I could think about while I sat at the fancy hotel's lounge bar sipping a terrible dirty martini and waiting for him to show up.

It had been a little over a year since we'd shared a cab and curiosity had gotten the better of me once again. I hadn't even planned on staying in the city this long, let alone having a causal fuck buddy for a few nights every month when our busy work schedules aligned.

Seth: Drinks?

That's how it always started. Once he was in town and got a little lonely—or more like horny—one word sent me running to him.

Him. Even the thought of his abs and captivating blue

eyes was enough to soak my panties and make me want to make every bad decision possible. Add in his husky voice and impeccable style and you had sex on a stick just waiting to be licked and sucked.

I could see him from the corner of my eye. He was watching. Waiting. Playing our little game perfectly.

Sitting at the bar, sipping on my drink, I caught the eye of a man in his mid-twenties across the bar. He looked to have a swimmer's build and was fairly clean cut.

He'll do.

I bit my lower lip once, knowing both men were watching. Slowly licked my teeth. Sipped my drink and licked the rim of the delicate glass.

Hook. Line. Sinker.

Swimmer-boy took the bait like a smallmouth hiding under a log on a hot summer's day. He slowly made his way over to the empty seat next to me.

"This seat taken?" A brogue soaked his words, fucking sexy as could be.

I shook my head no. "All yours, Sir Wallace." I sipped slowly on my drink, trying not to choke on the bitterness hitting the back of my throat or the cheesiness of my Braveheart reference. He was making me nervous. The way he smiled as he slid into the seat next to me sent my heart racing.

"Sir Wallace, I could get used to that." He laughed a deep throaty chuckle. "Not from around here are you?" His bright honey eyes raked over my skintight jeans, down to my high-heeled boots, and then up to my tits, which were about to pop out of my tight fitting silver tank top.

"How'd ya guess?" I winked at him, playing with the toothpick that had held my blue cheese stuffed olives.

"Call it a hunch." He took a swig of his beer and waved the empty bottle to the bartender.

"You have good instincts. I'm Savanna." My lips turned up at the corners when my watcher tugged at his tightening suit pants.

It's working.

"And does Sir William go by another name?" I ran my hand over his toned bicep, under his loose fitting cotton shirt.

He cleared his throat. "Finn. It's nice to meet you Savanna."

I leaned in closer as the bartender set Finn's new beer in front of him. "So what brings you stateside, Finn?" His name felt good rolling off my tongue. For the first time in a year another man had lit a fire in my belly. *Dang it.* I was still here with someone else.

"I've been here since college. My sister and me came here to chase the American dream."

Damn his voice was intoxicating.

I looked over to where my watcher had been, now an empty table. Time to snap out of the Irish love spell Finn had enchanted me with.

A cough came from my other side and I shot a seductive smirk over his way. "Hello?" I cooed as he took a seat next to me. "It must be my lucky day. Two hot men at once."

He winked at me before looking over to Finn. "Savanna here is taken." His husky voice thumped with possession and my heart raced a little as his hand caressed slowly up my thigh.

Finn got up and without a word walked back to his seat at the other end of the bar.

"He went quick," I remarked, pushing a lock of hair behind my ear.

"Savanna, is it?" He licked his lips and bit down hard.

"Yes, sir. I am in town on a visit."

"Is that so? Well I'm Clayton." He extended his hand to mine. Once my hand was firmly in his grasp, he pulled me in close to him, wrapping his other arm around the small of my back to scoot my chair close, right in between his legs.

"Nice touch, changing your name, Joey. It's sexy." He kissed right under my ear on the nape of my neck.

Chills. Fast electrifying chills coursed throughout my hungry body.

"Wanna get out of here, Clayton?" The new name felt bitter and exciting escaping my mouth as our fingers intertwined.

Tonight is going to be fun.

He helped me off my stool. Even in my six-inch heeled

boots, he was still a good five inches taller than me. His face was stubble-ridden from his late night work meetings and early mornings at wherever-the-hell-he-worked, but his dark hair was trimmed perfectly into a military style crew cut. I figured him to be an ex-marine, but our relationship never got to details like that. I knew he worked out a lot, had no tattoos, and loved extra dry martinis. That his kiss was enchanting and he fucked like a sex god on steroids. That he lived in some suburb of Boston, but was from Florida originally. That his real name was Seth Roberts. And that's it.

He knew my first name, how to make me weak at the knees and come within seconds. He knew what building I lived in and that I worked as a freelance photographer.

The casual nature of our relationship made it easy to not get too attached, but I was addicted. He was a drug that I barely got to play with but craved most nights. And right then he was going to be mine.

We started to head out of the bar, passing Finn. "Bye, Will." I smirked at him as a questioning look crossed his face, making me giggle a little to myself.

He's a rodeo I'd love to ride.

The martini was starting to get to me; even one and I was a little tipsy. They called people like me two beer queers where I came from, but I didn't mind being a lightweight.

We walked through the marble lobby, got in the elevator, and attacked.

Seth pressed me up against the mirrored wall, pulling

my leg onto his hip. He lightly bit from my collar bone to my chin while I slowly rubbed his growing erection. He growled into my neck, making my clit pulse with need.

"God, it's been too long." I huffed into his ear as he reached up my tank top and under my bra, tugging on my nipples just the way I loved it.

The elevator slowed, forcing us to pull away from each other until we were behind the closed door of his suite.

I went right to the bed, slipped off my boots, and stripped down to my bra and panties.

Seth groaned as he watched me slowly undress from the other side of the bed where he was already standing in his birthday suit, stroking his erect member leisurely. "Put your boots back on. Never leave them off, Jolene. Never."

"Yes, sir." I did as he asked then got on my knees on the bed, staring right at him. I slowly started to massage my breasts over the lace, playing with my nipples, watching how his dick pulsed in reaction.

"You like that?"

He nodded.

"And this?" I ran my middle finger under my panties, over my soaking clit, slowly biting my lower lip out of sheer pleasure. A low rumble came from the back of his throat.

"Fuck. You're so damn hot. Come here."

I got off the bed, went around to where he stood, and did what he wanted before he could speak the words.

I took his girthy nine inches into my mouth until it painfully stabbed the back of my throat.

His fingers curled into my hair, pulling my head back. "Look at me. The. Whole. Time." He thrust into me and I gagged, never breaking eye contact.

His cock felt so good.

Hurt so bad.

I loved it.

He thrust harder and harder into my mouth until tears formed in the corners of my eyes. That's what got Seth off the best: knowing it was painful. Right as his dick started to throb, he released my hair.

"Get on the bed. On your knees and put your hands behind your back."

I faced away from him, hearing him open and close the nightstand drawer quickly. Handcuffs bound my wrists and clicked to the tightest setting they could.

"Painful?"

"Just enough."

"Good."

He pressed his chiseled chest against my back, letting his cock slide between my cheeks snuggly. "I want your ass, Joey. Can I have it?"

"You can have whatever you want."

Quickly, he spun me around and shoved my head down next to his dick. "Get it nice and wet. We don't want to go in dry, now do we?"

I spit and sucked until he was more than lubed enough to enter. I turned away from him again and quickly my face was on the bed, my ass high in the air and my black thong pulled down to right above my knees. His hands spread my cheeks and he spit on my backdoor. Slowly he put two fingers in.

I moaned and he pulled them out. "How was that?" His husky voice was coated in lustful desire.

"Fucking amazing," I moaned into the comforter.

"How about this?" Forcefully, he thrust three fingers in and out of my opening, pushing in as deep as he could, stretching me, getting me ready.

I moaned and he spit again.

"More," I cried.

Without warning pain and ecstasy shot through my body as he thrust his cock into my ass as hard as he could. Through sighs and growls he panted, "Did you bring them?"

I nodded as well as I could with my face smashed into the comforter. "My bag" was all I was able to mutter before a pleasurable scream escaped.

"Fuck. Your dick is amazing." I sighed as he slowly pulled out.

Seth got off the bed and grabbed my purse to get the

tiny pink vibrator out of its silk bag, along with a thick leather belt and a condom.

Still in the same position, Seth's hand gently grazed over my bare ass. "You've been running."

I nodded.

"Your ass is fucking gorgeous." He nipped at my left cheek quickly with the belt, sending a slap into the air. I cried out. Pain was pleasure, such fucking amazing pleasure.

I could feel him start to unlock the cuffs. "Leave them," I begged.

"As you wish." His voice was gravelly with lust.

He rolled me onto my side, laying down behind me. He put the unwrapped condom in my hand and rested his hard cock on my fingers. I fumbled with the latex until it slid down his shaft. I lifted my leg and waited anxiously for his dick to finally fulfill my desire to have my pussy filled with his beautifully talented cock.

I heard the vibrator buzz to life and I moaned just from the sound.

"Tease," I pouted.

"Beg."

"Please, Seth. You know you're driving me crazy. Fuck me the way I like it. Please." I sounded like a fucking school girl on her prom night. I hated when he made me beg but I knew it got him harder and that was usually my main goal.

Slowly he started to rub the small bullet over my swollen bud. Gentle little circles swirled me into a frenzy that I could barely think straight through.

I stuttered, "Ple-please—Seth—fuck!"

Finally, his dick rested in between my slick folds, lightly putting pressure on my opening. I wanted his dick pressing onto my g-spot so badly, my entire body ached. Right as his cock started to fill me, my knees started shaking. He leaned back and grabbed my bound hands, thrusting harder and harder onto the perfect spot.

I cried out loudly as I felt my climax building in the pit of my stomach. "Fuck—Seth—I'm going to come."

He pumped harder and faster while my pussy tightened around his length. His dick twitched with his own climax coming on fast. One hand's fingers laced into my hair, pulling back hard as the other gripped around my neck perfectly.

God-fucking-damn-it.

I shook as a light layer of sweat coated my body. I could feel the pulsing of his dick pump harder as his release matched mine.

Slowly our bodies came out of our orgasms and our muscles relaxed. He released my wrists from the cuffs and kissed the top of my head sweetly.

"Fuck, Joey. That was..." His head hit the pillow as I threw my boots onto the floor on top of my crumbled clothes and pulled one of his white undershirts over my head.

"Yeah, amazing as usual." I curled under the covers into his arms and drifted off into a post-sex coma.

CHAPTER 3.

"Babe?" I kissed Seth on his prickly cheek as he grunted at me. "Come shower with me?" Only one eye opened with an eyebrow raise.

Grunt. Snort. Roll over. Bury face.

"I guess that's a no."

I climbed out of bed, slowly stretching out my back, which was tight from sleeping on the hotel's pillow top mattress. It was too soft for even Snuggle to be comfortable on.

Slap! The sound of Seth's hand striking my bare ass right as I was about to make my way across the carpeted floor rang out through the suite.

"Fuck! Seth!"

He rolled over to shoot me a devilish grin. "It's too perfect to not!"

I chuckled and grabbed the white plush robe out of the closet. Seth started to snore softly again, his face buried under his pillow. I watched him for a second before heading to the bathroom.

It only took a few minutes for steam to start engulf the marbled space. I scrubbed my body and hair in honey-melon hotel shampoo, used Seth's razor to quickly shave my legs, and was out of the shower as fast as possible—I was hoping there was time for a quickie before my lunch with Brett.

The feeling of a smile spread quickly as I thought about my amazing cousin. He was one of the kindest, most confident, and most hilarious people I'd ever known. After my parents decided to ship me off to boarding school for being a "black sheep", Brett was the only one in the family that kept in contact with me. I was bred a southern belle but didn't live up to the title. The old money that was stained in oil dripped from most of my family. It was wrong, but I reaped the benefits too, and just tried my best to not let it consume me too much.

With the robe cinched tightly around my waist, damp hair pulled up into a messy bun, I ambled back into the room. Seth was sitting on the edge of the bed, staring at his phone with his brow creased, looking completely distraught.

"Everything ok?" I took the seat next to him and tried to nibble on his neck only to be swatted away.

"You have to go. Something came up." He gripped the sides of his cell, barely taking in breaths.

"Alright." I grabbed the pile of clothes from the floor

where I had tossed them the night before. My thong and jeans were successfully on when the door swung open. Not thinking about it, I whipped around, bare-chested, pissed off, and ready to scream at the intruder for not heeding the "do not disturb" sign.

"What! The! FUCK!" The words rang out like a shrieking poison from a gorgeous pregnant woman standing in the doorway. "Seth! You damn two-timing jackass."

I grabbed my shirt, pulled it over my head as fast as I could, and threw my bra into my purse. "Well, this is fucking terrible," I muttered, standing awkwardly in the middle of the room. Every cell in my body was begging me to bolt, but Mrs. Douchebag was taking up the entire doorway.

Seth stood by the bed, gaping—freaking chicken shit that couldn't even defend himself. I guess there wasn't much to say. He had been caught with another woman.

Oh for fuck's sake! I'm the other woman. I should be mad too!

"You're fucking married?" I yelled, turning to the coward as he gasped for breath. All he could do was nod and continue to stare at his now sobbing wife. She looked to be just about my age and very pregnant, like too pregnant to even be traveling.

"Chloe, what are you doing here?" His shaky voice crackled in the air.

Pathetic.

"Well, I think I should go. For what it's worth, I am so sorry." I gave a sympathetic smile to the woman and tried to get past her. She moved just enough for me to squeeze by then whispered, "I hope you're happy, slut!"

"What the hell?"

Ugh! Damn my tongue.

I took a step back and pointed at the rat bastard in the middle of the room. I hissed, "I had no idea that your husband was married. He never wore a ring. He never talked about you. If he had I would have freaking bolted. I am not a slut. He is. I am sorry you're married to a man-whore and have his spawn festering in your belly, but that is not my fault."

Slap.

Wow, that hurt.

Seth's face boiled while his chest heaved.

"Fuck you!" I yelled as I kicked him right in the balls and marched out.

It was the worst walk of shame of my life. No bra. Boots in hand. Rummaging through my purse to make sure my vibrator and belt were where they were supposed to be.

Fuck!

I turned on my heels and slammed the door to the room open. With two pairs of devil eyes glaring at me, I dove under the bed. Thankfully, that's right where my pink o-maker had rolled after Seth was done using it the night before.

I shoved it back into my bag, smoothed out my clothing, and left again. Chloe and Seth were yelling at each other while I was waiting at the elevator, texting Brett to meet me at my apartment so I could wash the shame off of me. I heard Chloe scream, "Oh God! My water broke."

Well, I am not fucking hanging around to see this.

I ducked into the staircase and hoofed it down the fifteen flights barefoot.

What a fucked up morning.

"Wait, so she went into labor?" My cousin sat on my sea foam corduroy couch, sipping his mimosa while Dozer laid his big head in Brett's lap.

"I guess so. I didn't stick around to find out!" Painting my nails on the floor, I tried to laugh about the terrible morning I'd had. "So fucked up, right?"

"Yeah, that shit only happens to you my dear." Brett was wearing a loose white dress shirt partially tucked into his designer jeans with gaudy turquoise jewelry and accents. He had always been a better, flashier dresser than I was and way more glitzy. It worked for him, and it matched his personality well.

"So, how's everything going on the Tony front?"

Brett bit his lip, playing with Dozer's pointy ears. "There's a new busser at work that I have my eye on now."

"Oh yeah?" I loved Brett's escapades.

"He's eighteen. Just moved to the city. He needed a place to crash for a few nights so he has my pullout."

"You would. How straight is this one?"

"He thinks he's straight as an arrow, but I think there are a few kinks in that shaft." My cheeks flamed as Brett winked at me. Even though I was completely fine with his sexual preference, the fact that he was able to sleep with so many straight men was astonishing to me.

"Oh, so the real reason I wanted to see you is one of my friends is an author. She has two perfect models for her cover but her photographer has the flu. Are you free to do a quick shoot for her?"

"Maybe. Sounds like a fun project. When?"

"They want Central Park at dawn, sooner rather than later. She's on a time crunch."

I groaned. "That is freaking early as shit! But, yeah, I'm in. Luckily, I just have to roll out of bed and do the shoot."

"Thanks love. Her budget is a little tight."

"That's fine. I'll take whatever she was going to pay her other guy. If she's a friend of yours, I don't mind helping out."

"You're awesome!"

"Don't forget that!"

"I'll text her your number."

"Sure." The smile that spread on my cousin's face was adorable. He was the sweetest person in the world.

Brett stopped petting Dozer to fill up our mimosas so naturally, Dozer started his deep throaty grunt. "Your dog is so weird."

I whistled and Dozer plopped down next to me. I rubbed his neck with my elbow while blowing on my wet deep plum nails. "He just doesn't like it when the petting stops."

"Apparently." Brett rolled his eyes at my brown and white goofball, who was now panting in my ear while slapping his tail uncontrollably against the leg of the coffee table. "So we could set up a meeting for tomorrow with Kathy, my author friend. Maybe her models could join and we could talk about the shoot?"

I nodded. "Sounds like a plan. Set that shit up and order some Chinese. I'm starving."

"Chinese and a mimosa? You're a strange one."

I shrugged. "Yeah, but you still love me."

CHAPTER 4.

The next morning, I was woken up by Dozer softly grunting in my ear. His paws were on the bed and his face was only inches from mine. His entire body shook from his tail furiously wagging when he noticed that my eyes were opening.

"Guess someone needs a walk."

Walk—that pesky magic word that sends dogs into a tizzy of excitement. Dozer was no exception to that rule. He bolted to my bedroom door and started doing spin move after spin move, all too excited to venture into the busy hustle and bustle world of Manhattan.

I glanced over at my clock. I had two hours before I had to meet Brett and his author friend for brunch. I pulled on a pair of yoga pants and laced up my sneakers after scrubbing off all the makeup from the day before and throwing my hair up into a loose ponytail.

The sun was shining into my living room from my balcony so nicely; it was the perfect morning for a quick run with Dozer. I shot off a quick text to Brett as we walked out the door.

> **Me: Taking Dozer for a run. Can we go somewhere dog friendly? I want to bring him to brunch.**

> **Brett: Sure. How about the place right down the block from you? They have the best brioche French toast in town and we can sit outside.**

> **Me: Perfect. See you there in a little while.**

Dozer and I set off at a pretty good pace on our normal route in the park. Since it was Sunday morning, Central Park was crawling with joggers, tourists, and artists, and most of the benches were taken around the Alice in Wonderland statue. Dozer slowed and pulled me right to the bushes so he could sniff and pee on almost every branch.

"What kind of dog is that?" That voice, that accent—it was so familiar.

I whipped around to see a guy, just about my age, standing a little too close for comfort. Dozer, of course, trotted over to him, tail wagging. What a great protector he was.

Then I noticed them: the soft, gorgeous, honey colored eyes from the hotel lounge. Sir William Wallace in the flesh.

Shit, I forgot his real name.

"Savanna, right?" His voice was so silky. His eyes were so stunning. His jaw was so ridged. He was so attractive.

I shook my head. "I lied. It was roleplaying." My face immediately flared hot as the words left my tongue.

Way to go, very smooth!

"So that dick really was your boyfriend." His lips pulled down in a frown. A light layer of sweat was covering his reddened face; it was clear he had been out for a morning jog, too. His soaked gray shirt clung to every muscle while his chest heaved slowly.

"Not exactly. He turned out to be a cheat."

"Sorry to hear that." The way his lips turned up at the corners told another story.

Dozer nudged his leg and grunted. "Oh, this is Dozer. That means he wants you to pet him."

Sir Wallace knelt down and started patting him on the back. I cleared my throat. "I'm Jolene. Most people call me Joey. And he's a bull terrier."

"He's a cool dog." Sir Wallace got back to his feet. "Well, again, I'm Finn. Still just Finn. It's nice to actually meet you, Joey."

"You too."

"Maybe I'll see you around?"

"If you run Sunday mornings, you probably will."

With that he took off jogging, quickly glancing over his shoulder to wave goodbye at me. I pulled Dozer's travel bowl out of my backpack, gave him a little water, and then started to jog toward my meeting. Finn's eyes were all I could picture the entire time. They were freaking gorgeous.

I took a seat at an outside table and tied Dozer to the table leg. I was about twenty minutes early, but that was typical. I would always rather be excessively early than even two minutes late.

Me: Just got us a table. Are you almost here?

Brett: Be there in ten minutes. The models and Kathy are running a little behind.

Me: That's fine. See you soon.

"Can I get you anything while you wait for the rest of your party?" A sweet blonde wearing pigtails and bright pink lipstick leaned on the chair opposite me.

"A mimosa and some water for my pup?"

She nodded. "If you need anything else, just let me know."

I waved really quickly as she started to walk away. "Sorry, I forgot to mention that two more people are going to be joining us."

"I'll pull over a few more chairs for you and bring their menus over."

"Thanks."

She nodded, smiling sweetly as she dragged two more metal chairs across the brick patio. "Be right back with those drinks."

Brett was always a few minutes later than he said he would be so by the time he joined me, I had already finished my mimosa and was sipping on some iced green tea. Right when he sat down, my stomach growled embarrassingly loudly.

Brett laughed while pulling out his chair. "Sorry. I took a cab thinking it'd be faster than the subway. Traffic was a bitch."

"No worries, they haven't shown up yet." I motioned to the empty chairs in front of us.

Right then, a woman with fiery red dyed hair, probably in her mid-thirties, started making her way to our table. "Brett?" She called over to him with a wave.

Brett got up and gave her a hug. "Kathy, this is Jolene, my cousin I was telling you about."

I got up and shook her hand. "Nice to meet you, Kathy."

"Thank you so much for meeting me. I cannot believe— of all the weeks for my photographer to get the flu! The models were right behind me. Hopefully they'll be here any minute." She spoke with the slightest hint of an Irish brogue. Who would have thought I'd meet two people from Ireland in one weekend? Small world for sure.

We started to chat about where in Central Park we should do the shoot, what she was looking for in her pictures, the erotic nature of her storyline, etc.

"So, they need to be seductive and in love?"

She nodded, sipping on her cappuccino.

"Then wouldn't it be better for them to be in a bed, or at least in a bedroom? Maybe scantily dressed? In suggestively compromising positions?"

"That's what I originally wanted but my photographer talked me out of that."

I pursed my lips. That shit pissed me off. A photographer needs to get the right shot, not talk their client out of it.

My attention was quickly drawn away by a pair of gorgeous honey eyes staring at me as they got closer and closer to our table.

My mouth dropped open as Finn leaned over and kissed Kathy on the cheek. "Hey, sis." His voice was like molasses-coated sex. "Kiera isn't coming. She got called in for a shift at the diner," he stated firmly, taking a seat next to Kathy.

"Oh rats. Well, this is Jolene, our new photographer, and Brett, my dear, dear friend that I have told you about."

I got up to shake his hand. Finn stared right at me, his eyes wide like he didn't know how to handle this situation. "Hi, it's nice to meet you. We were just talking about where we should have the shoot."

The meeting went on while we gorged on French toast and I had two more mimosas. Dozer happily chomped on the rawhide I had brought to keep him distracted. Finn and I awkwardly avoided each other's glances. It was really weird.

Why didn't he say he knew me?

Should I have said something?

God he's beautiful.

"Alright, so it's decided. Y'all will meet me at my apartment 'round ten and we'll use my place for the shoot. I have a nice big four-poster bed and we can even use some props and really get into it. An erotic novel's cover should drip with sex."

"Jolene, you are brilliant! I don't know how I am going to be able to thank you for this."

"Referrals and repeat customers are always nice." I winked at Kathy as her face lit up with a huge smile.

For the most part, Finn had remained quiet through the entire meeting, frequently nodding and saying "yeah" a lot.

"Are you going to be ok with having Kiera almost naked on my book cover, little brother?"

Kathy looked kind of concerned when Finn shrugged and stated, "She dumped me weeks ago, so it's totally fine with me. I don't know how she is going to feel about it."

"Isn't she a model?" I knew tons of models and in the name of "the job" they understood that art was just that. As long as it was tastefully done, it shouldn't be a problem.

"I am, she isn't. She agreed to do this cover months ago when Kathy asked us if we'd do it."

Kathy put her hand on Finn's shoulder. "We'll make her

feel comfortable. It'll be fine."

"Well, this was great, but I need the rest of the day to deep clean my apartment." I laughed a little, trying to play off how I was trying to run away from Finn's enchanting stare. He was way too distracting.

Everyone shoved up from their chairs at the same time while I untied Dozer from the table. "See you in the morning." Kathy sighed with relief while hugging me tighter than necessary.

Brett kissed me on the cheek. "See you in the morning, cous!"

"You're coming?" My voice sounded more shocked than I intended.

Brett nodded quickly. "Seeing that piece of gorgeous Irish booty with his shirt off? Wouldn't miss it for the world!"

I glanced over at Finn, whose face was turning fifty different shades of red while he hugged his sister goodbye.

I laughed a little, waved goodbye to everyone one last time, and set off down the block toward my apartment with Dozer trotting happily at my side.

"Hey, wait up!" Finn jogged quickly down the crowded sidewalk to catch up to me.

"What's up?" I couldn't help up let my eyes wander over his gorgeous cheek bones and down to the abs that could faintly be made out under his tight fitting V-neck.

When did he have time to change?

38

I caught a whiff of his clean sent, which was complimented by a hint of cologne.

He had time to shower?

Suddenly, I felt like a slime ball.

"Have dinner with me tonight?"

I shook my head. "Sorry, you're a client now. I don't mix business and pleasure."

"Come on. My sister is your client, not me."

"Nope. Sorry. No can do."

I wanted to say yes. My body was screaming for me to say yes. Why were my lips betraying me and sticking to my rules? This guy—this hot freaking guy—was just the perfect person to break the rules for, and there I was turning him down.

"Bollocks. Well, lucky for you I don't give up that easily. I always get what I want—eventually." He winked. "See you tomorrow morning, Joey."

Before I could say anything, he turned and headed the opposite direction of my apartment. His ass was perfectly shaped in his jeans.

God, even his ass is gorgeous.

What the fuck is wrong with you Jolene?

CHAPTER 5.

Bang! Bang! Bang!

What the?!

Bang! Bang! Bang!

My eyes peeled open while the blaring red numbers from my nightstand screamed that it was freaking six thirty in the morning.

Bang! Bang! Bang!

"Fuck! Coming!" I yelled toward my front door. Whoever the hell had decided to show up at my home that freaking early in the morning was in for a rude awakening! That shit was not going to fly.

Dozer was planted next to the front door, wagging his tail and growling.

Bang! Bang! Bang!

"What?" I shouted as I flung my door open.

I was met by those stunning honey colored eyes I now recognized immediately.

Finn was standing in my doorway wearing athletic pants—the kind that make swooshing noises with every step, a tight fitting gray Under Armor shirt, and sneakers with a hanging bag draped over his right shoulder.

The small smirk that raked across his face while I stood there seething in my robe and pink slippers, makeup smeared all over my face and my hair probably a poof of tangles and curls, made me want to deck him right on the spot.

"How'd you…? What the…?" I was completely confused, leaning down to pet Dozer as he nudged my bare leg with his wet nose.

"I thought you might want to join me for my morning run." The smirk was still firmly planted on his face as he leaned against the doorjamb, looking way too perfect for how early it was.

I shook my head. "Do you know what fucking time it is, Finn?"

He looked down at his watch and then back up to me. "Damn we're late!" He winked and shoved past me to enter my apartment.

"What the hell do you think you're doing?"

He placed his hanging back on top of my dining room table and shrugged. "Putting my stuff down so we can go on

41

that run."

Dozer sat down at his feet and grunted until Finn started petting him on the head. "You're not going to take no for an answer are you?"

Finn shook his head, looking good enough to lick from head to toe.

"How'd you figure out where I lived?"

"You gave your address to my sister for the shoot so obviously she had to give it to me so I'd be able to find it." Pulling out a chair, he slowly took a seat. "The park is going to start getting crowded. You should really get some running shoes on."

I huffed and stomped my feet, risking waking up my neighbors below me, but at that point I was just putting on a show. Honestly, he was too fucking hot to be mad at, even at the ass crack of dawn, and it was a little sweet that he'd showed up in the morning not to try to plow me down, but to spend quality time with me.

It took me all of five minutes to pull on athletic attire and scrub off my smeared makeup. Dozer was happily keeping Finn company in my dining room when I made my way back to them. "Alright, let's do this. We need to be back by eight to shower and finish tidying up this place for the shoot."

He nodded. "Sounds like a plan."

I clipped Dozer's leash onto his leather collar and we made our way to the stairs down the hall.

42

"So, why do you want a running partner today?"

Our voices echoed up the stairwell.

"It's nice to have someone else there to help motivate you."

I smiled. "Yeah, that's what this one usually does for me." I tugged on Dozer's leash a little while he panted and bounced down the stairs.

"He is a pretty awesome dog."

"He's the best."

"Your accent is stronger in the morning." His observation and derailment of the conversation startled me a little and I wasn't sure why.

"I never noticed." I shrugged, opening the exit into the main lobby of my building. "Hey, Frank, thanks for letting this guy in this morning."

My concierge looked up with wide eyes. "He was on your list for today, Ms. Abbott."

"It's alright. I'm just giving you a hard time. We're off for a run. If Brett, Kathy, or anyone else on my list comes early, let them know that we'll be back soon."

"Of course." Frank's tired eyes and weak smile were obvious in the bright morning light.

The street was already hustling with commuters on foot and in cars blaring horns. We patiently crossed the street and started to jog into Central Park.

"It's a beautiful day," Finn called me to from a few feet ahead.

I picked up my pace to run alongside him, Dozer practically glued to my right flank.

"So where are you from exactly?" he continued. I hated talking during runs, which was why Dozer was the perfect running mate for me, but Finn seemed to want to be a chatty Cathy this morning.

"Mississippi."

"You're a long way from home."

"That's the plan." I was huffing. Man he could run fast. My heart was racing, my ears were pounding, and my breath was catching more than I would have liked. Thankfully, Dozer decided it was time for a pee break and diverted to the bushes.

Finn stood next to me while Dozer did his business. "I was born and raised in Clontarf. It's close to Dublin."

"And you came here for college?"

"Aye. I wanted to get more hotel experience and try to get into modeling, hopefully see some of the world. New York seemed like perfect place."

"It is good for modeling, I guess."

"You don't like it here, do you?"

"I never thought I'd stay in the city for longer than a year, but then my career took off and I travel so much that this is a pretty great hub. Do I like it? Not really. I'm not really the city type. I'd love to have a yard for Dozer to run and play in. Someday I'll move to Tennessee or the Carolinas."

"It is beautiful there. I'm actually doing a shoot in Boone, North Carolina, next week. I leave in a few days."

"What's the shoot for?" We started to jog again, but this time Finn let me set the pace.

"A toothpaste ad for some magazine. Work is pissed that I am taking off again."

"Work?"

"I'm one of the assistant managers of that hotel we met at the other night."

I glanced down at my watch. "We need to start heading back. Want to grab some coffee on the way?"

He nodded and we started to double back toward Starbucks. We didn't talk the rest of the way and even though I didn't mind the silence, getting to know Finn was entertaining to say the least. My crazy work schedule and the giant chip on my shoulder usually made it hard to make friends. It was a nice change of pace.

"What do you want?" Finn turned to me while I filled Dozer's travel bowl with water.

"A grande double white mocha and a lemon scone, please."

"Coming right up."

The door to my apartment shut behind us. With our coffees still in hand, Finn decided to shove me against the wall. He grabbed my paper cup, bending down to set in on the floor faster than I could register what was happening. Next thing I knew, his lips were attacking mine and his fingers tangled in my hair, which I just had released from its ponytail.

I panted as I pushed him away. "Finn, I told you. I have rules and this can't happen."

My body was betraying me: my heart was pounding, my clit was throbbing, and I could feel the need pooling in my yoga pants.

Finn took a step closer to me. "Some rules are meant to be bent, like this." He gently kissed my lips and I started to melt. His brogue, his touch, his eyes—it was all taking over my better judgment.

"Some rules are meant to be broken, Joey. Just like this." He scooped me into his arms. Instinctively, I wrapped my legs around him, letting him press me against the wall next to my front door.

"Let's get cleaned up for the shoot." His breath was hot on my neck as his whisper swept into my ear.

I sighed into him, kissing his soft lips again. "Ok."

How could I not give into him?

Fuck. My. Life.

He was just too beautiful.

He carried me all the way to my tiny bathroom, which felt extra cramped with both of us occupying the space. While the water warmed, we tugged at each other's clothes, practically ripping them off.

I yanked down his boxer briefs to reveal the most beautiful cock I had ever laid eyes on. It wasn't the biggest I had ever played with but it took the cake on perfection. He was at least eight inches, thick and pierced right through the tip with a simple barbell.

Holy crap, I need to ride that bucking bronc.

We climbed into the shower, breathing heavily in between desperate hasty kisses. I reached down, not able to wait any longer to touch him. Slowly, I started to stroke and he moaned at my touch.

"Joey, you're breathtaking."

His words shocked me. They were genuine, not just dirty talk like I was used to. They felt better than I could have ever imagined.

Quickly washing my hair and rinsing it out, Finn grabbed my body wash, put some on my pink loofa, and started to wash me from my neck, down my chest, all the way to my throbbing bud. Tingles ran through my body at his gentle touch as I slowly continued to play with his glorious manhood.

Once I was sufficiently covered in bubbles, I took the loofa from Finn and started to return the favor. His hands ran down my body, helping rinse off the suds before his fingers slipped slowly between my folds. He gently rubbed circles over my aching clit while biting my neck gently.

My body shuddered at his touch as he plunged deep into my wetness.

"Like that, beautiful?" His voice was low, his lips brushing against the sensitive skin below my ear.

I nodded, rubbing down his perfect abs to get the soap off him.

"I want you," he growled. Electricity shot through me.

Right as I turned off the water and the idea of tackling Finn's soaking wet body onto my bed filled my mind, Brett's voice called through my apartment, "Jolene? You here?"

"Shit," I muttered, throwing a towel around my body and hastily hopping out of the tub. "Get dressed quick. I'll be right back."

I dove out of my bathroom, throwing a towel around my dripping wet body. "Brett? You're early."

He had a paper bag in one hand and a holder with two cappuccinos from my favorite bagel place in the other.

"Thought you might need some help tidying up the place, and some breakfast." His eyes darted to Finn's hanging bag on the table and looked up and down my practically exposed body. "Is this a bad time?" An eyebrow raise and sly smirk quickly jumped onto my cousin's face.

Just then, right on freaking cue, Finn glided into the

room. Yeah, freaking glided. He was toweling off his damp short hair, shirtless with his running pants low on his hips. A coy grin spread quickly as he took in the shocked gasp that leapt from my throat.

"Oh my." Brett's hand flew to cover his laughing mouth as red spread from his ears down his neck. "He's hotter than I thought!" Brett's whisper was loud enough to fill the apartment.

"Finn?" I crossed my arms over my chest, trying to keep the loosening towel from dropping to the floor.

"My clean clothes." He pointed to the hanging bag. "You should get dressed, too, beautiful. Kathy just texted me, she's almost here."

My cheeks burned, but him calling me beautiful again was worth the awkwardness of the situation. I started to follow Finn into my room right as a knock came at my door. "Don't say anything?" My pleading eyes met my cousin's just as he was about to open the door for Kathy.

"About what?" He winked and called through the door, "Just a sec!"

CHAPTER 6.

I slammed the door to my bedroom shut and spun around in a fit—right into Finn's rock hard chest. His arms wrapped around me while I started my mild freak out.

"What in the hell was that?" I tried to shove out of his arms with no success.

I could feel him chuckle softly, pressing me harder into his smooth bare skin, which smelled like my coconut body wash. "I'm not ashamed of the fact that I think you're incredibly sexy and that your cousin witnessed my quasi-walk-of-shame."

I growled. It was the only sound that I could make without yelling and I could hear Kathy and Brett talking in the other room. There was no way I wanted to call attention to my tantrum.

"What is your plan for being locked in here with your sister out there? Not to mention your ex is about to walk through that door, too."

He let me go and with me went my towel. He knelt

down, kissed my bare stomach softly, and slowly looked back up to me. "I don't really give a flying fuck."

Kissing all the way back up my body, he sent chills down my spine while running gentle fingers over my hips and up my sides. His lips landed on mine like a butterfly on a daisy in summer, effortlessly brushing over them while whispering, "Just let it go, love. It's going to be alright."

I stood frozen in place, naked, staring into his eyes. Those beautifully gorgeous, stunning honey eyes.

A knock broke through my daze. "Hey are you almost done straightening up, Joey?" Brett's voice was muffled through the door.

"Just a second."

I ran around my room, throwing the covers back onto the bed, putting my hair into a bun, motioning to Finn to get his freaking clothes on, and finally grabbing faded skinny jeans and a loose fitting black yoga tank. No time for pleasantries like a bra, makeup, or doing my hair—they'd just have to deal with it. I hated that I wasn't wearing makeup but there was nothing I could do about it at that point and, quite frankly, that was the least of my worries. Finn looked incredible in a fitted white crew neck and dark washed jeans, the slightest hint of stubble lining his jaw from not shaving that morning.

He squeezed my hand gently. "I promise to be on my best behavior."

With a sigh of relief mixed with nerves, I gripped the handle. "Here goes nothing."

I opened the door to find Brett and Kathy on the couch sipping freshly made hazelnut coffee out of my favorite mugs, Dozer happily squeezed in between them.

"Finn, you're here already. I was just about to text you."

He rubbed the back of his neck. "Er, I went for an early run. Joey was nice enough to let me clean up here so I didn't have to go all the way back to my place."

"Oh, how sweet." Her kind eyes landed on me while I nervously grabbed our Starbucks cups off the floor next to my front door and set them on my kitchen counter. I noticed how much less of an accent Kathy had than Finn, more subtle hints of a brogue laced in her words where his speech was soaked in it.

"It was nothing, really. Is the other model on her way?" Right then a light tap landed on the front door as it opened and revealed one of the most stunning women I had ever laid eyes on. Her golden hair bounced with big barrel curls, her lips were a perfect red hue with a slight shine of lip gloss, and her eyes were a brightly piercing ice blue. There was not one blemish or freckle on her high, tanned cheek bones, she was tall and slender, and her curves looked perfectly proportioned under her navy maxi dress.

"Sorry I'm a tad late." Her voice was sweet, singsongy.

Damn it all to freaking hell—she's stunning. How can I compete with that?

The ugly bite of jealously got the better of me while I stared at her sashaying into my living room. Yeah, I didn't truly understand what sashaying was until Kiera waggled her hips perfectly to move her wedge-heeled, pedicured feet, bouncy boobs, and perfectly sculpted ass into my apartment.

"That's quite alright, we just finished getting Joey's room straightened up." I felt Finn's body close behind mine as his strong hand landed onto my shoulder and squeezed gently.

Kiera's eyebrow rose as she extended her hand to me. "Joey? Like Dawson's Creek?"

I feigned a giggle. "My name is really Jolene." If I had a dime for every person that had mentioned that reference to me over the years, I'd be freaking rich.

Her lips pursed together. "Nice to meet you, I'm Kiera."

I slid my hand into hers and felt all eyes on me. It was one of the most uncomfortable moments ever. "It's my pleasure." I swallowed hard.

This is going to be one hell of a shoot.

You're a professional—act like it.

"Shall we get started?" Kathy rose from my couch, setting her mug down on the coffee table.

"Sure." I bit my lower lip and motioned back toward my bedroom. "Come on in."

With everyone—including the panting Dozer—on my heels, I made my way into the bedroom. It was nothing special by any means, but for a Manhattan apartment, my bedroom was quite large. My off-white, king size, four-poster bed was smack dab in the middle of the dark hardwood floor with a soft lilac on the walls. Black and white landscapes that I'd taken in college hung with a giant mirror over the matching oversized dresser. Simple, very chic, not really *me*, but it worked. The bright pink and black paisley comforter did scream "Joey" and so did the matching area rug that was tucked under my bed.

Once everyone was in and the lights were set up perfectly, I took a long slow breath in, exhaling through my nose with my back to the crowd. "All set. Kathy, I put white sheets on the bed, would you like me to take off the comforter?"

She glanced over the bed slowly. "I love the pop of color. Let's try some with the comforter on."

I nodded. "Sounds good. Finn, Kiera, let's start with you guys about to kiss standing next to the bed."

Finn glanced at me, a killer smirk planted on his lips. "Shirt on or off, love?"

I gulped as his perfect abs crossed my mind. "On for now. Just so I can get a feel for what I'm working with."

And to help me gain my composure so I can concentrate on something other than how badly I want to feel that barbell that's hiding in your pants.

My cheeks flared as I shot Kiera raking her gorgeous fake nails down Finn's chest and back. They kissed each other's necks, cuddled, embraced. When Kiera started to pull Finn's shirt up over his head, jealousy hit hard in my stomach, but I fought through the terrible urge to tackle him onto the bed and mark my territory.

He's not yours to claim.

Sigh. He was stunning, laying back on my bed as Kiera climbed on top of him, my flash lighting up his perfectly toned muscles, his honey eyes, his enchanting smile.

"Cous?" Brett was getting up from the arm chair in the corner of my room. I had started to forget that he and Kathy were in the room watching me drool over Finn. Luckily, Kiera was was captivated too and therefore oblivious to my stares and glares.

He's her ex.

He's her ex.

She is an ex.

She's not standing in your way.

"Yeah?"

Brett cleared his throat. "Don't you have some *props* they can use?"

Ugh. Yes. Damn it. That was the last thing I wanted to see: Finn using my belt, rope, and scarves on another woman.

"Oh that could be fun." The excitement in Kiera's voice was way over the top.

"I do. Kathy?"

"Let's give it a try. With the comforter off, maybe?"

One sharp breath in.

This is going to be interesting.

I dove under my bed to grab my box of erotic toys. It wasn't too embarrassing, it's what I was into, I just wasn't thrilled with the fact that this was how Finn was going to find out about my kinky side.

Getting the cuffs, belt, and rope out as fast as I could, I slammed the lid shut before anyone saw my vibrator, cock rings, box of condoms, or the anal beads. Holding it all up, I looked over at Finn, letting lust drip into my southern drawl. "Pick your poison, Sir Wallace."

He bit his lower lip and his eyes lit up—exactly the reaction I was hoping for.

What the hell just got into me?

Professional. Keep this professional.

"Belt." The simple word whipped through the air and all I wanted was to be in Kiera's place.

I handed my thick brown leather belt over to Finn, our eyes locked on each other. My heart was racing. My breath was heavy. I wanted—no, I needed Finn to use that belt on me.

"What do you want me to do with it?" Finn's eyes never left mine.

"Put it around her neck?"

I glanced to Kathy and she shrugged. "That might be hot. I could add a scene with it into the book."

"I think I am going to need a copy of that." I tossed a smirk over my shoulder to Kathy with a wink.

An excited smile spread wide. "I'm sure that could be arranged."

Finn got onto his knees and pushed Kiera softly onto the bed so he was behind her. Wrapping the belt around her neck, he glanced up at his sister. "Good?"

Kathy nodded. "I think we found a winner."

"Yeah?"

Thank God this is almost over.

"I don't know how to even begin to express how much I love this," Kathy gushed as she looked through the pictures on my camera.

"I'm glad. I guess that's a wrap then?"

Kathy beamed as she glanced up from the digital screen. "Yes, Joey. That's a wrap."

I put the belt and other things back into my box and slid them safely back under my bed. "I can have the images to you by the end of the week, edited and everything."

"Brilliant!"

Kiera straightened out her dress as she shoved up from my bed. "This was a lot of fun."

Finn didn't even acknowledge her. He put his hand on my shoulder and locked eyes with me as he asked, "Got a sec?"

I glanced around the room before muttering, "Sure."

We walked into the living room. "Have dinner with me

tonight."

Yes! Say yes!

"Is that really a good idea?"

Why? Why do you always do this, Jolene? Stop playing hard to get!

"Yes, beautiful. I think it is a fantastic idea."

"Alright." I exhaled slowly. It was relieving that even after that intimate shoot, Finn wanted to be around me and didn't want to try to rekindle the flame that was sparking in Keira's lustful glances, caresses, and tone.

"I'm out of here, call me later?" Speak of the devil, Kiera's hand was on Finn's shoulder. It wasn't until then that I realized how close Finn and I were standing, not even an inch away from each other.

He took a step back and looked at her. "Now why would I do that?"

Her face quickly contorted into a pissed off mess. "What?"

"You heard me, Kiera. Don't forget who dumped who and where the door is."

Ouch. Apparently, Finn was not one for second chances. *Good to know.* She turned on her heels and stomped out of my apartment in a huff.

Kathy and Brett joined us in the living room.

"This was incredible. I loved watching you work, Joey."

Brett's smile was contagious as he stroked my ego a little.

"Thanks!"

"You really have talent, young lady." Kathy grabbed her bag off the couch, looking up at Finn. "Want to grab a bite to eat with your sister?"

Shoving his running clothes into the bottom of his hanging bag, Finn twisted around to look at her. "Yeah, alright."

"Thank you again, Joey." Kathy was halfway out the door already.

"Don't mention it! I'd love to do it again sometime."

With Finn, not Kiera.

"See you later, beautiful." Finn kissed my cheek and followed his sister out the door.

"See you later?" Brett had his hands crossed over his chest, his hip popped out.

"We're having dinner tonight."

"A date? That's not like you."

I shrugged. "Yeah, but he's different."

Brett laughed. "You mean he's incredibly sexy."

I plopped down on the couch and started to rub Dozer's white belly. "There's that, and there's just something about him. He really is different."

"Whatever you say, cous. I'm glad you're moving on from that two-timing asshole. He wasted a year of your life."

"Thanks? I'm going to pretend that wasn't a slap in the face."

He slouched down next to me and flicked on the television. "It was said with love."

"I guess that's all that matters."

CHAPTER 7.

I must have dozed off for a bit because I woke up to Dozer's wet nose nudging my arm insistently. I groggily rubbed my eyes, threw off the thin blanket that I usually cuddled with while I watched Teen Mom 2—my guilty pleasure—and patted Dozer's egg-shaped head. The sun was setting over Central Park and the view from the sliding glass doors to my balcony was breathtaking.

Shit!

I checked the clock on the wall: it was almost seven. I heard a knock on my door.

"Who is it?" I was too short to see out the peephole of my door. Dozer planted himself at my side, grunting and wagging his tail while he waited patiently for me to let our guest in.

"Finn, love."

Swoon.

My palms were instantly sweating as a giddy smile raced across my face and butterflies crashed around in my stomach.

I turned the lock and opened the door, completely ashamed at my lack of preparation for our date. Finn was wearing dark jeans, an untucked light green button down, and a sport coat—a perfect look for him. He had shaved his face clean of stubble and a fresh sweet musk of cologne filled the air.

"Now I feel underdressed. Come in."

He put his hand on my hip, brushed a kiss against my cheek, and slid inside the door. "You're stunning just the way you are."

Where did this guy come from?

"Want a glass of wine while I freshen up? I dozed off on the couch for way too long."

Usually in situations like this, I would be panicking, scrambling around my apartment to get ready, and rushing out the door. But Finn didn't make me feel nervous or late. Instead, his calmness emanated throughout the room.

"That'd be lovely." He followed me into the kitchen.

"White or red?"

"What are you drinking?" He pressed his chest lightly against my back as I reached for a wine glass off a high shelf in my tiny kitchen. His hands gripped my hips, his lips contacting the base of my neck as he took a deep breath in, stopping me dead in my tracks.

It took me a second to register that I still needed to answer his question. "White, I guess. For now."

I turned in his arms, his eyes piercing mine. "Then white it is."

I grabbed the half empty bottle from the fridge, poured our glasses, and leaned on the counter. I took a long sip of my favorite pinot grigio. The sweet, crisp apple lemon took over my entire mouth as I savored the quick moment.

"So, what's the plan for tonight?"

Finn's lips curled up at the corners. "Don't have a plan, really." He leaned up against the counter, pulling me by the hand into him.

"You asked me on a date with nowhere in mind?"

"Now what's the fun in that?" His lips brushed my ear, his breath warm on my neck and shoulder. "What do you feel like?"

I had no idea. I was expecting him to take me to his favorite restaurant where we'd sit in a poorly lit corner booth in the back, sipping on wine and losing track of time while we chatted about nonsense, lost in each other's company.

What romance movie dreamland am I living in?

"I'm up for anything."

His muscled flexed against me as he pulled me just a little bit closer. Finn's breath caught as he planted small kisses

63

down my neck to my collarbone. His fingertips dug into my hips. Goosebumps spread over my arms and my nipples stood at attention under the thin fabric of my yoga top. Trailing up under my shirt, Finn's gentle touch landed on my bare breast.

A low growl came from the back of his throat. "I love that you're not wearing a bra."

"I haven't had one on all day," I blurted out. *Smooth. Real smooth.*

"I noticed." His voice was husky.

Our lips connected, but only for a second. Finn pulled away slowly. "Go get freshened up. Wear something comfortable. I have an idea of where we should go."

I made quick work of doing a simple smoky eye, taming my long hair, and putting on a pair of black skinny jeans, a bra, a light teal blouse, and my ostrich boots. After grabbing a blazer and dabbing on a touch of Victoria's Secret perfume, I reentered the living room.

"Ready?"

Finn was on the couch, feet up on my coffee table, Dozer rooted to his side with his head in Finn's lap.

"Yeah." He downed the last of the wine in his glass. "You look wonderful."

I grabbed my keys. "See you later, buddy." I kissed Dozer on the head and we made our way down to the lobby. After grabbing a cab and heading to the Upper East Side, we made our way down the block to a restaurant that I had never even heard of before.

"Where are you taking me?"

Finn grabbed for the door handle, holding it open for me. "You'll love it here."

We walked into the narrow bar where most of the high top tables and bar seats were already filled. Live music was emanating from the back of the restaurant, some kind of Irish folk music. An older bartender waved to Finn and pointed to a table right next to the bar that was being cleaned off by a busser.

"Come here often?"

Finn led me to the table by my hand and helped me into the high seat. "Actually, this was the first place I worked when I came to the States."

The bartender made his way over to our table. "Finn, it's good to see you."

"Hi, Johnny, this is Joey."

Johnny took my hand and kissed the back of it swiftly. "It's a pleasure, Joey. What are ye havin'?"

He handed me a menu, which listed all of the bottled and draft beers they offered and had a logo at the top that said "Doc Watson's". "Oh, I'll take a Magner's please."

Johnny nodded and looked over to Finn. "A pint of the black stuff, Johnny. Thanks."

"No problem. Be right back."

"Black stuff?"

Finn laughed a little. "In Ireland, black stuff is Guinness. I just ordered a glass of Guinness."

The music picked up tempo, bringing a whole new feel to the old wood-covered bar.

"This place is pretty great."

"Aye." Finn looked around. "It's like home."

"Do you ever want to go back?"

Finn shook his head. "I like living here. Besides, there's nothing to go back to over there."

"No family or anything?"

Johnny set the drinks down in front of us. "Anything to eat?"

Finn ordered us a lamb burger with goat cheese and fish 'n' chips. Without missing a beat, he took a sip of his beer and answered, "Kathy's all the family I got left."

Well this got serious fast.

The sweet cider covered my lips as Finn took my hand. His eyes were slightly glassed over while he sat in thought.

"I'm sorry I asked."

Finn shrugged. "That's life, you know. Nothing to be sorry about." He paused for a moment. "So tell me about that guy at the bar. What happened?"

"Why would you want to know about that?"

Finn started to lace our fingers together. "Well, I thought you might want to talk about the difficulty of having just been cheated on. If you do, I'll listen, but if not, I understand."

I laughed a little at the ridiculousness that had unfolded only days before, though it felt like it had been months at that point. "Actually, I was *the other woman*."

"Oh jeez." Finn's lips perked up at the corners as he stifled a laugh. "Now, that's a shame."

"Why's that?"

"Because no one as incredible as you should be anyone's secret. You deserve to be loved out loud."

I leaned over the table, eyes closed as I reached for his lips, but air and a coughing sound were all I was met with. I opened my eyes to see Johnny standing next to our table with the plates of food in hand as I was leaned halfway over the table. I could feel my cheeks and neck prickle with heat as Finn chuckled in front of me.

"Thanks," Finn said to Johnny as he set the food in front of us, smiling sheepishly at me.

"Enjoy."

"Well, that was awkward." I popped a fry into my mouth.

Finn leaned over the table and I met him halfway, his lips full and soaked in his milky beer. It was pure electricity, more so than I had ever felt, and it was just a simple peck of a kiss. Just as quickly as it started, it ended, and my butt was planted back on its stool. I devoured the most delectable lamb burger I had ever tasted. Come to think of it, it was the only lamb burger I had ever had, but it was surely not going to be my last.

Feeling overly stuffed and like a complete pig, I gulped down the bottom of my second Magner's and beamed over the table at Finn. "This has been great."

He nodded, waving at Johnny for the check. "It really has been terrific."

Johnny came over with the folded bill in his shirt pocket and another round for us in hand. "Just one more, on the house. For old times."

"Thanks, Johnny." Finn handed him a few bills out of his wallet. "Keep the change."

After taking a quick drink from his glass, Finn had a foamy Guinness stash dripping on his upper lip.

"You, uh, have..." I pointed to his lip and we both busted out laughing.

He wiped it away with his paper napkin. "Good?"

I nodded, still giggling a little. "Yeah, you got it."

"So today was...interesting."

I rolled my finger around the rim of my glass. "Interesting is definitely a word to describe it."

"How would you describe it?" His eyes were locked on

mine, suddenly smoldering as he licked his bottom lip.

"Frustrating. One of the exact reasons why I make it a point to not mix business with pleasure."

"But don't you remember, breaking the rules can be simply brilliant." A devilish grin crept onto Finn's lips as images of our shower together popped into my head.

"I do remember."

CHAPTER 8.

"That was a lot of fun." I locked the front door, throwing my purse onto a dining room chair.

His hand landed on my hip as he started to follow me into the kitchen. "Why do you sound so surprised?"

"I normally don't do dates." I started to pour wine into our glasses from earlier. "Want to stay for a nightcap, Will?"

"Sure." He kissed my lips briefly. "I'm glad you made an exception for me."

I reached up, quickly kissing his gorgeous mouth. Hunger took over. I needed more than just that fleeting moment of connection. I smashed my lips to his, wrapping my arms around Finn's neck. Soft moans escaped the back of my throat as his tongue feverishly explored my mouth. My body immediately started to react to his seductive, intoxicating touch.

Finn effortlessly lifted my ass onto the cool marble counter as he started to unzip my jeans. I bit down on his neck as his fingertips connected with my swollen, slick bud. The slow, gentle circles made me shudder and twitch instantly.

"That feels…" I let my head fall to his shoulder as the pleasure took over. It had been so long since something so simple had consumed me that much. I felt the beginning of my orgasm build in my stomach as I pushed him away slightly.

"Too much?" Finn's brow creased.

"I just want to play too." Kissing him deeply, I sucked and bit on his lower lip before jumping off the counter.

I knelt down, taking his jeans with me. Lightly, I kissed along his boxer line over his defined lower abs, which made the sexiest V I had ever seen—pure sex lines leading the way perfectly.

While slipping my fingers under the elastic of Finn's boxer briefs, I suddenly got nervous. With one hand, Finn knotted his fingers in my hair, pulling my head back to make me look up at him. The other tugged down his underwear. His hungry eyes watched my every move, his tongue slowly rolling over his bottom lip.

Finn's flawless cock was at the perfect level. I rolled my tongue over the barbell, never breaking eye contact. Gingerly, I worked my way down his shaft, licking and kissing. His subtle groans cheered me on as I took him down into the back of my throat, taking my time, sucking gently, rolling my tongue over the tip.

Without warning, Finn's grip on my locks tightened, slamming his cock farther into my mouth. I choked a little and moaned. I pulled away, just enough to let it happen again.

"Fuck, you're incredible."

His dick started to throb—he was close.

Finn released my hair, grabbing my shoulder to pull me to my feet. Hastily, he undressed, throwing his clothes on the floor in a pile. I immediately followed suit.

"Condom?" I looked up at him, trailing my fingers up and down the perfect dick that I could not wait to have deep inside me.

"My coat."

I dug in the inside jacket pocket, ripping the foil package with my teeth and sliding the thin latex over him. His breath quickened as he engulfed my mouth with his. Desire pulsed between us as he shoved me against the wall, lifted me into his strong arms, and let his dick press on my aching cunt.

"Just take me, Finn. Don't hold back."

A low rumble emanated from him as he bit down on my collarbone. "I can't stop thinking about that belt."

"Then let's go get it."

With me still in his arms, Finn headed back to my room. I glanced over his shoulder to see that Dozer was snoring softly in his bed in the living room. I laughed a little to myself.

"What's so funny?"

"Oh, nothing. Just the fact that my dog doesn't even care that we're home. Some great protector he is." I rolled my eyes and lightly brushed my lips against Finn's muscular shoulder.

Finn shut the door to my room with his foot and set me down on the bed. "Maybe he just knows you don't need protecting from me."

He put his hand on my shoulder, gently guiding me to lie down. His lips wrapped around my nipple, letting his teeth gently play for a second. My back tensed as I gripped my comforter. It was shocking how quickly my body went into an ecstasy overdrive from the most simple of caresses from Finn. It was a euphoric reaction that had never happened to me before.

"Be right back."

I propped myself up on one elbow to see Finn dive under my bed to grab the box that held my most intimate of playthings. I had never had a guy know about the entire stash before, usually only bringing out the particular toys that I wanted them to use to retain a little control over the event.

His voice was pleasantly smooth as he gripped the belt in one hand and my pink o-maker in the other, one eyebrow raised slowly, a sultry smirk landing on his lips. "Get on your stomach, love. It's my turn to play."

I scooted up on my bed and rolled over onto my stomach, gripping a pillow comfortably in my arms. His fingers trailed over my cheeks as a growl escaped his lips. The bed dipped on either side of me as Finn straddled my lower back, barely putting any weight onto me. He looped the belt around my neck, pulling it tight.

"Is that ok?"

I nodded, biting my bottom lip.

He leaned back onto his heels, gripping my hips firmly. Pulling my ass into the air, Finn lightly tugged on the belt. My breath quickened as chills shot down my spine. Suddenly, he let go of the belt, pushing two fingers into my soaked pussy. He rolled his fingers around until he hit my spot perfectly, making me cry out.

"Does that feel good, Joey?"

I moaned into the pillow. "So. Fucking. Good."

"What do you want?"

He pulled his fingers slowly out.

"I want to feel you inside me, finally."

He shifted behind me, grabbing the end of the belt again. "As you wish."

His erection filled me in one swift thrust of pure pleasure. Finn wasted no time: he was fast and rough, pushing farther into me with every thrust. His barbell pressed against my g-spot flawlessly, sending shooting chills over my entire body.

"Holy freaking..." My knees were shaking. Finn's left hand gripped my hip bone and pulled me harder into him. His balls were smacking gently onto my pulsing clit. The belt applied the perfect balance of pleasure and pain that I craved so much.

Quickly, my release started to crash over me, my hips bucking into Finn as he groaned and his cock pulsed deep inside me.

With a heavy sigh we both collapsed onto my bed. Finn took the belt from around my neck as I started to catch my breath.

Finn's honey eyes locked on mine. "That was incredible."

I rolled onto my side, Finn pulling me into his arms. I felt my vibrator roll into my leg and I grabbed it. "I think we forgot something."

Finn softly smiled, kissing my forehead. "There's always next time."

"Who said I was going to invite you back for a *next time*, Sir Wallace?"

He shifted under me, pulling my hips onto him, gripping tightly. "Because you enjoyed that as much as I did."

I leaned down and nibbled a little on his neck. "You're probably right."

I could hear Dozer lightly scratching at the door. I sighed. "As much as I don't want to leave this bed, I really need to walk him."

"Let me clean up a bit and I will go with you."

I got up from the bed. "You don't have to."

Finn shook his head. "The park isn't that safe at night. It'd be my pleasure."

"Thanks."

He stopped in the doorway of my bathroom, watching me pull my shirt on. "Besides, I'm not ready for tonight to be over."

Walking through Central Park at night always seemed magical to me. The quiet streets and trees gently glowed under the street lights as we walked hand in hand with Dozer bouncing at my side.

"So, when is your next shoot?" Finn's voice was low and husky as his brogue soaked the air.

"I leave to shoot a wedding in Nashville in a few days. What about you?"

Dozer bolted into the bush next to me after a squirrel, yanking me away from Finn. Trotting to get back next to us where Dozer was grunting at the base of the tree the squirrel had escaped up into, Finn took the leash from me. "Here, let me."

Dozer quickly lost interest and we continued back toward my apartment. "I leave tomorrow afternoon for five days."

Thinking about being away from Finn, even for just a

few days, bothered me more than it should. "That'll be fun."

He shrugged, wrapping his free arm around my waist. "It would be better if you could come with me."

Leaning into his shoulder, I sighed. "That's the nature of the beast. Our work schedules are bound to clash."

We stopped in front of my building, the doorman holding the door open for us. "Coming up?"

Finn handed me Dozer's leash, shaking his head. "I would love to, but I have laundry to do before I leave. I really need to get home."

His hand softly landed on my cheek as he pulled me in for a tender goodbye kiss.

"Text me?" His words were barely audible.

I nodded. "Sure."

I smiled and stared as Finn went to the curb and hailed a cab.

CHAPTER 9.

The next day I spent most of my time glancing down at my phone, hoping that Finn would call or text. I felt like an idiot, but he had really done a number on me.

After running with Dozer twice and not seeing Finn in the park, cleaning my apartment again even though it didn't really need it, and giving Dozer a bath, I decided that it was time to stop waiting for him to contact me.

Me: Have a safe flight, Sir Wallace.

Finn: Just boarded. There's an empty seat next to me, wish you were here.

How cheesy can one guy be?

Me: I'll see you when you get back. We'll make up for lost time.

Way too forward. What is wrong with you, Joey?

Finn: Can't wait.

I started to flip through the channels of terrible daytime television when my cell buzzed on the coffee table. Brett's face was smiling bright on my screen.

"Hello?"

Brett's cheery voice came through the other line. "Lunch in fifteen?"

"Sure. Sounds great."

Brett and I decided to order Chinese and lounge in my apartment instead of going out. Fifteen minutes later on the nose, Brett walked into my apartment and the tantalizing smell of General Tso chicken wafted into the air.

"Alright, girly. Spill." Brett was barely in the front door and he was already diving into the third degree.

Taking the bags from him and returning to the living room, I took a deep breath. "Let's have a little wine first."

"That good? Or that bad?" Brett went into the kitchen and grabbed the wine out of the fridge and glasses from the cabinet. I just smiled at him.

We sat Indian style around the table, eating with our chopsticks right out of the takeout containers. After a few sips of wine and delicious pieces of spicy chicken, Brett forced a cough. "I'm waiting pretty patiently over here." With a wink he popped a snow pea into his mouth.

"Fine." I couldn't help the smile that sprang onto to my lips as my cheeks and neck tingled with blush.

"Oh, this is going to be good."

I nodded. "He's pierced."

Brett sat up straighter, setting down his to go box. "Like Prince Albert or Jacob's Ladder?"

"Like right through the head on the top."

Brett's face turned a bright crimson as he pictured Finn's manhood in all its jeweled glory. "How amazing is it?"

"Simply perfect. *He's* perfect."

"Wow. I never thought I'd see the day or that it would happen this fast."

"What?" Dozer started to nudge me, begging for a piece of chicken.

"That you'd fall for someone. I always pictured us being roommates and having five dogs in the Village."

I threw my napkin at him. "That's mean. Besides, you have your sexy couchmate bus boy to settle down with."

Brett pursed his lips. "He got fired and I had to kick him out."

"What happened?"

"Well, he got promoted to server because we had a few people quit. Great, except that idiot was bringing fake money as his bank into the restaurant. He'd give the customers a few real and a few fake bills as change, always small. He got it mixed up the other night and gave a cop a fake five. He got arrested right on the spot. Haven't heard from him since."

"That is terrible."

"At least I didn't have to call the cops myself, he did make it kind of easy on me."

"True."

I saw my phone light up on the couch with a text.

> Finn: Just landed, beautiful. Hope you're having a great day.

> Me: Have fun and let me know how the shoot goes.

> Finn: I'll call you tonight after my meeting with my agent.

> Me: Sounds good, Will.

> Finn: Are you ever going to stop with the Braveheart references?

> Me: Do you want me to?

> Finn: No, I like being compared to a heroic Scot with great abs.

> Me: Oh, I got the country wrong, huh?

> Finn: No matter, love. I'll still think of it as a compliment.

Brett set his glass down a little louder than he needed to, snapping me out of my daze of texting Finn and ignoring my company.

"Sorry."

Brett laughed. "No biggie, but thanks for driving my point home."

I sighed. "He really is amazing."

"I'm glad. You're worth it."

His saying made me smile. He used it as a justification for almost anything. If I wanted an expensive pair of boots or a day at the spa, he'd always talk me into it by saying I was worth it and deserved to spoil myself.

Later on that night, right after Dozer and I got home from our walk and got comfortable on the couch, my phone started vibrating in my pocket. Butterflies started to attack my stomach as I read Finn's name lighting up on the screen.

"Hey."

"Hello, beautiful. How was your day?"

"Uneventful, you?"

I could hear a door shutting behind him and keys hitting a table. "Just got back from my dinner meeting. I'm beat. Traveling always takes it out of me."

Dozer started grunting, upset that I wasn't paying attention to scratching behind his ear anymore. "Hush, bad boy," I scolded Dozer.

"What'd I do?"

"Sorry, Dozer's being a brat. Do you want to head to bed?"

"No, it's lonely here. What are you doing?"

"Sitting on the couch with Dozer." Thump, thump, thump. Dozer's tail started hitting the cushion at the mention of his name.

"You should climb into bed with me."

"Well, you're a little far away for that to happen."

"Pretend. Do what I say."

Chills.

"Ok."

"Let me know once you're in your room."

I practically ran to my room.

"Ok. I'm shutting my door."

Finn's voice got lustful. "Good, now undress."

I tugged at my clothes, leaving them in a pile where I stood.

"I'm standing in the middle of my room naked, just for you."

"Just the way I want it. Get your vibrator out and get comfortable under your adorable blanket."

"Ok, one second." I dove under my bed and threw the box open, grabbing my battery-powered boyfriend eagerly then cuddling under my plush comforter.

"I'm in bed, babe. Vibrator in hand."

Babe. The pet name rolled off my tongue so fluidly. *Too soon?*

"Put the phone on speaker."

Tap.

"Done."

"Roll your fingers over your gorgeous breasts."

A light moan escaped as I massaged my boobs.

"Pinch and pull on your nipples, love."

"Are you…" My voice shook a little.

I didn't even have to finish my statement before Finn answered, "Of course. Turn on your toy and slowly rub it on your gorgeous shaved cunt. Go slow. I want you to really enjoy this."

The buzzing noise started and my back tensed. I was no stranger to pleasuring myself, especially with my vibrator, but this was my first time having actual phone sex. The act had always seemed odd to me, but Finn was orchestrating my pleasure effortlessly.

Goosebumps spread down my legs as I groaned into the phone, "Oh, Finn."

"That's what I want to hear. Joey, get rougher, go faster." He was panting.

His growl emanated from the other line. "Fuck. Joey. I wish that was me making you shake and moan."

"Hurry home then." My climax rushed in fast. "Holy shit, Finn, I'm coming."

A moan rumbled deep in his throat. "Me too. Damn it, Jolene!"

I tried to catch my breath. "Finn, that was amazing."

Finn's voice was low as he murmured, "Just wait until I get home."

"Can't wait."

"Me neither, love."

I could hear him yawn.

"Why don't you get some rest? We'll talk tomorrow."

"Goodnight, beautiful."

"Night, Sir William."

CHAPTER 10.

A few days passed without me hearing from Finn. I kept telling myself that he was just busy shooting and to not worry about it. There was no way I was going to blow up his phone and seem like a stage five clinger, so I let it go.

When I landed in Nashville, I powered my phone back on and saw that I had a missed call and a message from Finn.

"Hey, love. Sorry it's taken me so long to call. The shoot has been really busy."

Some lady's voice was in the background calling Finn to hurry up.

"Work calls. Chat soon. Miss you, love."

Hearing his husky accent through the receiver made my heart putter. I shot off a text.

> **Me: Just got to Tennessee, call me when you get time.**

I got all the way to the hotel before a reply came through.

Finn: I'll try to call you tonight. Don't work too hard.

I set up my laptop and googled how far Boone was from Nashville. He was a five and a half hour drive away—a little too far to just drive to him, but I definitely thought about it.

I had a busy afternoon of meeting with the bride and her wedding coordinator followed by a boudoir shoot with her. I'd have the following day for touring the city or driving to Finn since the wedding wasn't until the day after. Originally, I'd been overly excited about taking in the country music capital's sites, but all of that excitement had flown out the window once I'd gotten love drunk on a sexy Irishman.

The shoot zoomed by with the most bubbly, adorable bride I had ever worked for. She'd had kind of the same upbringing that I'd had: old money that that she refused to let control her. Her mother would have freaked if she'd known that we were doing a sexy shoot for her husband to be, so she had to pay me in cash, which was totally fine by me.

After a nice long bubble bath in my suite's Jacuzzi tub, I slipped into my silk pajamas. I had fought the urge to call Finn for hours, but I desperately wanted to see if he would be up for me taking a day trip to Boone.

I gave in to my desperation and dialed his number. It rang three times before an unexpected voice came onto the line.

"Finn O'Shea's phone." A perky woman's voice startled me.

"This is Jolene. Finn is expecting my call."

"He's in the shower right now. Can I take a message?"

"No. No message. I'll try him later."

Click.

What the hell? Why was a woman answering his phone?

Well, that was that. Why would I have ever thought that Finn O'Shea would be any different from any other two-timing jerkface of the world?

The wedding had been beautiful, but I was so relieved to be walking through my apartment door. Dozer leapt off the couch where he had been sitting with Brett.

"Hey! How were my boys? I missed you!"

I got down on the floor without shutting the front door or bringing my bags all the way in.

"How did the wedding go?"

"It was a lot of fun. Great shoot."

"And?" Brett was standing over me, hand on his popped out hip.

"And nothing. I haven't heard from him since another

woman answered his phone while he was in the shower."

"Oh honey." He put his hand on my shoulder, plopping down on the floor next to me.

I rested my hand on his. "Oh well. That's what I get for trusting my stupid heart."

"Someday someone will be worthy of your love."

"I'm not going to hold my breath."

He kissed my cheek. "Well, I hate to run when you're mopey, but I'm going to be late for my shift if I don't head out. I walked Dozer twice already today, he was antsy without you."

"Thanks for staying here with him."

"Any time. Love you."

"Love you too."

I grabbed my bags out of the doorway and hugged my sweet cousin goodbye.

My phone vibrated in my pocket. I pulled it out to see Finn's name scrolling across the screen.

Nope.

I hit the fuck-you button.

I hope he can take a hint.

No message.

I brought my bags into my room, turned on the shower, and didn't even have my bra off before he was calling again.

I hit the fuck-you button, again.

He called again.

I guess he can't take a hint.

I got into the shower without ending the call. The pipes moaned, spewing out steaming hot water that engulfed the tiny space. I loved the way warm water felt rolling over my tired aching muscles. I loved what I did but being on my feet all day, climbing on chairs, and kneeling on mushy grass left me exhausted and sore the entire next day.

Turning off the shower and wrapping my plush robe around my dripping body, I made my way to the couch for a much needed TV-surfing-cuddle-session with my pup. Dozer hopped up next to me, nuzzling his head onto my leg while he shifted to get comfortable.

After a few *Happy Days* reruns, I started to nod off, until the sound of knocking came from the front door. I glanced at the clock on the wall: it was almost midnight.

"Who the hell?" I muttered as I went to the door, straining on my tiptoes to see through the peephole.

No luck.

"Who is it?" I reluctantly called through the door.

"It's Finn."

"Go home."

"Please let me in. I don't know what I did. Just talk to me."

"Ask the woman who answered your phone the other night."

"What? Joey, let me in."

"Are you going to go away if I don't?"

"Not a snowball's chance in hell."

"Fine."

I cinched the belt of my robe tighter and opened the door. It looked like Finn hadn't slept in a few days. His eyes had dark circles around them, his shirt was wrinkled, and stubble lined his jaw.

"So, why are you here?"

Finn followed me into my living room where I sat on the couch, letting Dozer lay between us.

"Because I lost my phone in North Carolina and I didn't get a new one until this afternoon. When you weren't answering me, I thought you were pissed that I didn't call you for a few days."

I laughed. "Don't pretend you care about me, Finn."

"What in the bloody hell are you talking about? Of course I care about you."

"Then who was it that answered your phone the other night while you were in the shower?"

Finn looked completely stumped for a few seconds, and then a light bulb went off. "Fucking Angie. My manager."

"Yeah, good one. It was late at night; she must be one hell of a manager." I rolled my eyes while Finn shot up from the couch, his eyes wide, hands in the air.

"We had been working late and had room service called up to my room after going over some of the photos from that day's shoot. I've never touched her." His brogue was thick as he spoke a mile a minute.

"Look, Finn, I'm not looking for excuses. We have no commitments or responsibilities to each other. Just don't lie."

He was too nervous; there was no way he was telling the truth. He sat back down next to me.

"God damn it, Joey! Just because you've been hurt before doesn't mean I don't feel committed or that I am not a bloody gentleman. Angie has chased girls away before, saying they were bad for my focus. I'm sorry. I should have suspected that she hid my phone and not assumed that a maid swiped it from my room."

"It's really convenient that your phone disappeared right after my call."

"I swear." He got up from the couch and knelt in front of me. "I like you." A coy smile danced onto his lips before he took my hand in his and continued, "You have bewitched me, body and soul."

"Now that is cheesy."

He bit his lip. "But it's the truth. Mr. Darcy was one smooth son of a bitch." His full lips pressed gently onto mine.

"Please believe me. I want you, only you. Promise."

"You think that quoting Jane Austen is the key to making me believe you?"

He nodded. "Is it working?"

I didn't know. Maybe he was different. He seemed different. Maybe it was me that was all fucked up and unable to believe that someone could genuinely want to be with me.

"I guess I just jump the gun a little when it comes to shit like that."

"I understand. I don't blame you. I would have been put off too." His fingers gripped the belt of my robe, casually pulling it loose. "Let me make it up to you."

Before I knew what to even think about what was happening, Finn was carrying me to my room and shutting the door behind us. He gently put me down on my bed, dragging the robe off my body and throwing it on the floor.

"Lay back and relax."

He pulled my knees to the end of the bed, letting my legs rest over his shoulders.

"I've been dying to taste you for days."

His kisses started slowly around my bald pussy, gently massaging my swelling bud with his thumb. Lightly he started to lick and suck on my clit, sending electricity shooting throughout my body.

I cried out, "I love how your tongue feels. Suck harder,

Finn."

He did as I commanded, and holy hell was he talented. Every flick of his tongue, every light nibble of his teeth, every suck from his lips sent shudders up and down my spine.

Groans and moans escaped as I gripped the sheets. "Fuck me, Finn. Please."

He pulled away from me. "I hope this isn't too forward, but I got you something."

I propped myself up to watch him walk out of my room. I realized I must have been too blinded by my frustration before to notice the paper shopping bag that he had in his hands now as he stared at me from the doorway.

"Well, what is it? The anticipation is killing me."

A shy smile perked up as he slipped a bright pink dildo out of the bag with a bottle of Her Pleasure lube.

"I thought this might be fun for us to try."

I raised my eyebrow. "I'll try anything."

"Good."

He hastily pulled off his clothes and his beautifully perfect cock was standing at attention for me as he knelt onto the bed. Finn took a small dab of lube, trailing it from my clit all the way to my ass.

"Are you on birth control?"

I nodded, a little nervous about where this was going.

"Have you ever done it without a condom?"

I shook my head.

"I haven't either."

"Fuck it. It's supposed to be freaking amazing."

Finn's lips crashed onto mine. I took the lube from him, got a small amount, and started to apply it to his hardening dick.

"Can I fuck your ass?"

"Please do."

He rolled onto his back, pulling me on top of him.

"First, I want to feel that gorgeous cunt around my cock again."

His wish was my command. I slid him into me and slammed my hips into him. His cry of pleasure cheered me on while I rode him, locking our lips.

"Grab my tits and bite me."

I trembled under his touch as his teeth sank into the tender skin of the base of my neck. After a few thrusts, I could feel his cock throbbing.

I pulled away from him. "Not yet. You still haven't told me the plan for that." I pointed over to the dildo.

"Turn around."

I did as he asked, positioning my ass right where he would want it. A soft buzzing sound started and prickles of excitement made the hair on the back of my neck stand on end. Finn reached around my body and held the six-inch vibrator to my clit.

"I'm going to fuck your ass while you fuck your cunt with this."

Yes. Holy-mother-of-all-sexual-ideas.

I lifted off of him, letting him slowly go deep inside me. Pleasure and pain spread quickly while I leisurely rocked my hips into him.

"Do it, Joey."

I angled myself and took a deep breath. The vibrating sensation filled me while Finn gripped my hips, pulling me into his thrusts as I was practically paralyzed from the euphoric ecstasy.

"Holy shit, Finn. This is..." I couldn't speak, my orgasm building faster than I wanted it to.

"Joey, your ass is so fucking tight. You feel amazing."

Only a few more minutes was all I could take. "Finn, I'm fucking coming," I cried out.

"Good, baby. Come for me."

His body quaked under mine as he pulled out and let his warm come shoot onto my back, my orgasm crashing over me like an electric wave.

I turned off the vibrator and started to get up.

"Let me." Finn scrambled to his feet and got a

dampened hand towel from the bathroom.

He sat on the bed behind me, kissing my shoulder as he cleaned my back. "You're incredible."

I turned to look into his gorgeous honey eyes. "So are you. I'm sorry I doubted you."

"It's ok."

"Can you stay tonight?"

He pulled me into him and laid back onto my pillows. "There's nowhere I'd rather be."

CHAPTER11.

The next morning I rolled over to find that I was alone in my bed. A sinking feeling started to creep into the pit of my stomach as I heard my front door slam shut. I grabbed my robe from the floor and made my way into the living room to see Finn setting coffee and a bag of bagels on the dining room table.

"Morning, love." He made his way over to me, planting a kiss on my forehead. "I took Dozer on a little stroll and grabbed breakfast on the way back."

"You didn't have to do that."

He handed me my favorite coffee. "I know. I wanted to."

We sat down for our breakfast, Dozer chomping on his rawhide in the living room.

"When is your next shoot?" Finn looked across the table at me.

"Actually, today at your hotel."

"Brilliant, I'm working at noon."

I took the last sip of my coffee. "I have to be there at four."

"Hopefully I'll be able to see you, as long as we're not too busy."

"Will I see you after?"

"You're not getting away from me that easily, not after last night." He winked and I blushed.

"Good."

The large ballroom was packed with excited guests as they filed into the rows, awaiting the ceremony. I was busy snapping candid shots of everyone while my partner for the day was off with the bride doing her first look shots with her dad. Usually that was my favorite part, but I had been brought onto this shoot last minute because the original second photographer had broken his hand in a rollerblading accident while I was in Nashville. So, I didn't have much say in what I did, I was just along for the ride.

An all too familiar voice broke my concentration and I got rigid. "Joey? Is that you?"

I turned around and, to my horror, saw Seth standing there in an expensive suit, without his wife on his arm or a ring on his finger. "Where's the wife and baby, Seth?"

He rubbed the back of his neck, taking a step closer.

"She left me," he whispered.

Shocker.

"Good for her. Now if you would excuse me."

"I've missed you."

"I'm working."

He shoved his hands into his pockets. "Alright."

Thankfully, he took his seat—right next to where I was standing, but at least I could move away from him, which I did in a heartbeat.

The night rolled into the reception. Finn must have been really busy because he hadn't made his way into the ballroom to check on things like he had planned.

Out of the corner of my eye I could see Seth standing next to the bartender, staring at me while he sipped on his martini.

"I'm going to run to the restroom." I looked over at my partner for the evening. She gave me a quick nod and I bolted to get a little bit of privacy. I heard the door close behind me as I came face to face with a sloshed Seth. He was standing inches from me, his hand wrapped around my wrist.

"You're so pretty," he slurred.

"You smell like a bar. Leave me the fuck alone."

He threw me into the wall, his body weight pinning me in place while I squirmed to get free. He tried to kiss me and I reached up with all my might and slapped him across the face.

"Oh yeah, baby. I know you like it rough."

He shoved me again and I screamed, "Seth, you're a fucking dirtball and you need to get the hell off of me right now!" Panic started to break into my words.

The door to the bathroom opened, revealing an enraged Finn flying across the room and connecting his fist to Seth's jaw. A few seconds later security guards burst through the door and started to restrain Seth.

"What do you think you're doing interrupting me and my girl?" Seth grumbled, trying to break loose.

"She's never was and never will be yours." Finn was seething.

"Who the hell do you think you are?"

"The man that loves the woman you just tried to rape, you filthy fuck."

I slouched to the floor, heaving hysterically, tears flowing down my cheeks. Without a word, Finn scooped me up and carried me down the hall into a vacant room.

He cradled me in his arms and sat down on the couch, never letting me go. He wiped the tears from my eyes. "You're safe, Joey. I promise."

"Did you mean it?"

Finn looked at me questioningly. "Mean what?"

"That you love me."

His kissed me tenderly, pulling me closer to him. "Yes. I

101

know it's fast but there's just something about you that I know I never want to live without."

"I love you too, Finn."

"Wait here." Finn started to get up from the couch, handing me the remote.

"Where are you going?"

He kissed my lips quickly. "To let them know why you're not working the rest of the night and to get excused from the rest of my shift."

I started to follow him. "I should really go home to Dozer."

Finn spun around and shook his head. "Call Brett, see if he can let your dog out. You're not leaving this room until I know that dirtball is far gone."

I nodded, sent a text to Brett, and slumped down onto the couch.

Finn returned in less than an hour, Styrofoam containers in hand.

"Hungry?" Finn's honey eyes were tired and worried.

"Famished. What'd you bring me?"

"A grilled chicken sandwich. Is that alright?"

My stomach growled. "Anything would be alright at this point."

We sat on the king size bed and chowed down on soggy

cold French fries and mediocre sandwiches.

"Everything alright with Dozer?"

I nodded, swallowing my last fry. "Brett's staying the night at my place."

"Perfect. Then we can stay here." Finn gathered the empty containers and pulled down the sheets.

"Are you sure this is ok?"

He grabbed my hand, helping me under the covers and into his arms.

"Joey, I promise this is alright. You had a rough night. Get some rest."

I shifted to try to get comfortable but my clothes kept bunching up. I sat up and started to undress.

"What are you doing, love?"

"I'm not going to be comfy with all this on."

He unbuttoned his shirt, pulled his undershirt off and handed it to me. "Here."

I yanked it over my head. "Thanks."

Once our pants were thrown onto the floor, Finn's arms secured around me again. "Goodnight, Jolene."

I kissed his smooth cheek. "Goodnight, Sir Wallace. My knight in shining armor."

He chuckled.

"What's so funny?"

"William Wallace didn't wear armor."

I shoved him gently with my elbow. "Whatever!"

"I'll still take it as a compliment even if your knowledge of history is shit."

"Night, Finn."

"Sleep well, my love."

EPILOGUE.

ONE YEAR LATER

"Baby, wake up." Finn's brogue broke into my dream-filled sleep.

"Five more minutes?" I tried to turn away from him, pulling the blanket onto my shoulders.

"We're about to land, Joey."

"Are you going to tell me what we're doing going to Nashville anyway?" I rubbed my eyes and returned my seat to its upright position.

"I told you, it's a surprise."

After Finn's photo shoot in Boone, his modeling career took off. He had been traveling all over the world doing magazine ads and was even starting to break into television commercials. With his busy schedule and mine, we were lucky to get one or two weekends a month together. When he mentioned that he wanted to take me on a surprise trip, I was thinking something more like Costa Rica or Italy, not Nashville. Don't get me wrong, I was very happy to have five whole days of quality time with Finn, no matter where in the world it was.

We grabbed our luggage, rented our car, and started to drive into the middle of nowhere in the mountains.

"Come on! You know I hate surprises!"

Finn glanced over at me from the driver's seat. "It's just down this road. We're almost there, beautiful."

We made our way down a long winding gravel road until Finn parked the car in front of a house that was clearly under construction.

"We're here. Come on, I want you to see something."

I climbed out of the car and followed Finn toward the unfinished home. He led me into the wood-framed structure and up the stairs.

"Are you sure this is safe?" He was leading me out onto a balcony that didn't have a railing set up yet.

"Trust me, I called the builder and asked if this was ok."

"How do you know the builder of this place?"

He grabbed my hand and turned me to look out at one of the most breathtaking sights I had ever seen. The rolling hills were covered in lush greenery and ran into a gorgeous mountain range off in the distance. There was a small garden in the backyard with tons of purple, pink, and white flowers of all kinds.

"So to answer your question, this is our new home."

I was shocked. I froze. I didn't know if I was mad that he had made such a huge decision without me or thrilled because he was finally helping me live out a dream of mine.

"I don't know what to say."

With that, he got down on one knee.

"Joey, I love you. I have since the moment I saw you in that bar. There is something about you that I never want to be without for one more second of one more day. Please, spend the rest of your life with me. Marry me, Jolene."

I heard grunting and sniffling coming from behind me. I turned to see Brett, Kathy, and Dozer standing on the balcony behind us, videotaping the proposal.

"Well, I think that handsome man asked you a question, cous."

I jumped into Finn's arms. "Yes! Of course."

He slipped the ring around my finger and pulled me into him. "Thank you," he whispered.

"For what?"

"For making all my dreams come true."

I kissed his soft lips and muttered, "Thank you for being my dream come true."

THE END.

DID YOU ENJOY WHAT YOU JUST READ?

RATE IT: If the answer is yes, you did enjoy Stupid Hearts, please consider putting up a review on **Amazon**, **Goodreads**, or **Barnes and Noble**.

SHARE IT: Please help spread the word about Stupid Hearts. Tell your friends and family about it or share it with them. Sharing is caring, after all.

STAY CONNECTED: Follow Kristen Hope Mazzola on **facebook.com/authorkristenhope** or **twitter.com/khmazz** to stay up to date about new releases, giveaways, and so much more! Also, join Kristen's email mailing list for her monthly newsletter: **www.kristenhopemazzola.com/mailing-list.html**

OTHER BOOKS BY
KRISTEN HOPE MAZZOLA

<u>Crashing Back Down (Crashing #1)</u>

<u>Falling Back Together (Crashing #2)</u>

<u>The Hysterics</u>

THE HYSTERICS

PROLOGUE

FAÇADE

FALLON

I was Fallon Dunbar.
I was a drummer.
I was confident, strong, and driven.
I was a junkie.
I am dead.

The full boxes scattered around my small one room apartment made it feel more real. The sinking feeling in the pit of my stomach made it feel so wrong. The new title and job made it feel surreal.

I am Fae Dunham.
I am the assistant editor of Raging Underground.
I am unsure, nervous, and scared shitless.
I am in recovery.

Staring into the full length mirror I had just hung up on the back of the door in my new room, I saw the shell of what I used to be, the life I could no longer have. The only traces left of my old life were the lip piercings I refused to take out. They were my favorites and they were staying. People like me don't get second chances, but for some reason, I was standing knee-deep in one.

There's no turning back now.

I will live again.

CHAPTER ONE

PRACTICE & MEMORIES

DANE

"Hey, man, you all right?" Colt was looking over at me from his seat on his amp.

I gripped the sticks a little tighter in my hands and shook myself from my zone-out. "Yeah. Sorry." I still couldn't get Fae off my damn mind.

Maverick tossed a bottle of water over my toms before swinging his bass guitar's strap back over his shoulder. "Let's take it from the top?"

My sticks clicked quickly, counting out the beat before sending Maverick and myself into a thumping bassline that shot goose bumps up my arms and legs. It felt like I was falling in love every time we started to play; it was *that* exciting.

Finally, the groove settled in nicely and we took off into our newest song, which I was sure would rock our show the next night. It took a while, but an hour and a gallon of sweat later, we were satisfied with how "The Lifespan of a Firefly" sounded.

"This is some great writing, Dane. Why haven't you given us lyrics before?" Rodney holstered the mic and took a swig of his seventh beer while his words slurred a little.

Grabbing a brown bottle out of the fridge, I tried to figure out an answer to his question that didn't make me sound like a complete pussy. "Never thought anything was good enough before, I guess."

Epic fail – that dripped vag all over the place. Way to have a backbone.

"Well, from now on, grow a pair and dish out more of this shit. It's gold. I think we should open with it tomorrow night for sure!"

Colt and Maverick both mumbled and nodded in agreement. My ego felt like it had grown ten times right there on the spot. Being the drummer, I never considered that writing lyrics was something I could be good at. Yeah, I was a journalist. Yeah, I had written angsty teenage poetry when I was younger. But I'd never considered myself an actual writer.

As I slouched onto the worn out couch in Colt's basement, memories rushed over me like warm acid rain.

Beer and sweat were all I could smell as I wiped my dripping forehead with my shirt sleeve. The gentle hum of the Russells' dryer slowly faded in, a little too soft after the booming of our last song left the air.

"Great session, guys." Maverick's weak smile faded as his words lingered in the space. We all knew and we all felt it, but we left it unsaid. There was too much, and no words could make it better; there was nowhere to begin. It was our first practice after the accident a few weeks before and the tension in the air was suffocating us all.

I nodded and choked out, "You guys think we're ready?"

113

Rodney laughed from the couch, gripping the mic in his hand. "We better be. Like it or not, we're opening tomorrow at Mountain Breath." His faded Zeppelin shirt was starting to wear a hole next to his collar and his lucky Chucks had mud caked on the sides.

"You gonna dress like a bum for it?" Colt joked, opening another beer we'd stolen from his old man's stash. Mr. Russell knew we took them but was usually too loaded to care.

Rodney threw a sweat-soaked towel at Colt right as I stood to stretch out the kink that had been building up in my lower back while I'd sat behind my faded burgundy Ludwin set.

"I think it's going to be sick," I muttered, trying to be enthusiastic and failing miserably.

Maverick clapped me on my back before starting to put his bass in its case. "You ready?"

Digging my keys out of my pocket, I stared at my sticks where they rested in their bag attached to my floor tom. I stood up gradually from my stool, starting to make my way to the stairs. "Yeah. Let's head home."

"Get a good night's sleep, gents! Tomorrow is going to be epic!" Rodney called up to us from the bottom of the stairs, a sly grin fixed firmly on his face. He had no fucking idea what he was asking of Mav and me, and it was better off that way.

The sound of a beer opening in my ear and the feel of cold suds spraying on my neck and cheek snapped me back to real time. Rodney erupted into a fit of laughter next to me.

"What the hell, man?" I thrashed, wiping my face off with the bottom of my shirt.

"Come on. I couldn't resist. You were zoning out again."

Colt sat in a metal folding chair across the faded lime green carpet, laying his guitar down next to him. "You all right, Dane? You've been spacey all night."

"Yeah, man. I'm fine."

I got up and started to make my way up the stairs to take a piss. Right as I opened the basement door, I heard Maverick say in a low voice, "Guys, it's April thirteenth. You know how he gets around this time."

My stomach sank. He was right. The twentieth was coming too fast for me to keep up with, and the memories and dreams were getting worse by the day.

Deep breaths.

Easier said than done.

Time would pass and it would still be hard, but I was still breathing.

Fuck it.

As I walked into the living room, trying to make it into the back hallway undetected by Colt's parents, I heard crying coming from the couch.

Turning on my heels, I found Sheila Russell sobbing into a pillow. When I cleared my throat, she popped her head up, startled by my presence.

"Sheils? You all right?" I looked down at Colt's kid sister, who was definitely not a kid anymore.

Before, she'd been pimply-faced, chunky, and awkward. Now, her face had cleared, she'd hired a personal trainer, and her degree in Mass Communications was helping her break out of her shell, to say the least. She was stunning in her own way. Not my type, but still pretty.

"Yeah." She sniffed. "I just got turned down for an awesome summer internship. It's the only one I applied for and that's biting me in the butt now." She tried to laugh it off, but her eyes stayed sad.

"You know the saying, Sheils."

She rolled her eyes and mumbled, "Don't put all your eggs in one basket."

I laughed, nodded, and gave her a tight squeeze as I continued on before my bladder busted. While I was trotting over to the half bath down the hall, Sheila called to me, "Thanks, Dane."

"Don't mention it! Call Julie. Schedule a mani-pedi date like the old days and you'll be good as new!" I yelled back before slamming the door shut behind me, barely able to get my zipper down before I pissed myself.

SNEAK PEEK

CRASHING BACK DOWN

Prologue

Excitement started to form butterflies in my stomach while Cali and I giggled in her bathroom, getting our makeup just right for our first adventure into the new world of college Greek life. We had met only a few weeks back during sorority rush, and we'd become instant friends. We could not have asked for more, being pledges for the same sorority and starting to dive right into a 'real' college experience. It was the first night of fraternity rush, and some of our older sisters had invited us to join in the festivities at one of the fraternity houses on campus. It was a really big deal, and we were bubbling over with giddiness.

When we were finally walking up the dampened front lawn of the frat house, I grabbed Cali's arm, completely in awe of the sea of ravishing men we were wading through. She pointed out an especially good-looking guy wearing his letters across his noticeably chiseled chest. He was tan and tall, and he had tattoos poking out from under his sleeves. I bit my bottom lip and salivated with Cali as we followed the hottie into the foyer.

There were tons of guys and girls, all grouped off, trying to convince potential new members that being Greek was amazing and that this was the fraternity for them. It did not take too long for a handsome brother to stride up to us, and to our surprise, the guy I had been mentally undressing before stood next to him. I found out that the hottie's name was Walker, but my attention was quickly diverted to his friend, Randy. There was just something about him that stunned me.

We chatted and flirted with them throughout the night while meeting other potentials who were not so favorable. Apparently, during fraternity rush, they had a few guys doing "trash duty," meaning any guy who over stayed his welcome was kindly escorted out by the trash handlers. It was a pretty fun role that Randy and Walker let us participate in. We drank, chuckled, and toyed. Cali and I played with our hair, laughed at every joke, and batted our eyelashes perfectly.

A pimply-faced freshman puffed on his inhaler while talking to Randy, and Cali grabbed my arm. "Come with me to the bathroom." I nodded and asked Walker where it was.

His lips curled seductively as he put his hand on the small of my back, pointing in the direction of the girls' room. "Don't worry, we cleaned it this morning." His Southern drawl curled around the words, making him that much more attractive as he winked and gave another sexy smile. We both fawned over his seductive tone as we weaved through the crowd to the bathroom.

Luckily, the oversized bathroom that smelled like piss and Lemon Pledge was empty. Cali undid her shorts and plopped on the toilet while I checked my mascara in the mirror.

"Those two are freaking hot as hell, Mags!" Cali's voice was full of excitement mixed with lust.

I touched up my makeup, trying to talk without messing up the liquid eyeliner. "The girls were right. There are men for the picking." I finished and turned to Cali, who was zipping up her tight black shorts. "Which one do you want?"

Her eyes went wide at my words. "Randy is all over you. Obviously he's yours! Besides, Walker has a bad boy Southern edge I'd love to jump on!"

I nodded, feeling my cheeks blush with anticipation and lust as I grabbed Cali's hand again to lead her back to find our evening's prospects.

I was thankful that the pimply-faced guy had already been booted by the time we returned.

Randy's eyes lit up a little when he noticed us walking toward him. He slid his arm around my waist and hugged me close to him as he handed me a fresh beer. "Having fun?" His silky, deep voice tingled in my ear while he whispered, sending goose bumps down my neck and arms.

Trying to be as sexy as I could, not really being the best flirt and so nervous to come off as an awkward freshman, I licked the top of the bottle a little before taking a long swig and then nodded. "Yeah, tonight's been great!"

Randy hugged me close again, a smile dangling on the corners of his mouth. Faintly a hint of red dusted over the back of his neck. Seeing the slight red creep over Randy's skin made longing surge through my body. Right then I knew I was in deep water already.

Toward the end of the night, another one of the brothers came over to introduce a brand-new pledge to Walker, claiming that he was his perfect match for a little brother. The five of us all got along like we had known each other for years. The conversation flowed easily between all of us, and we stayed together, laughing and joking for the rest of the evening. Mitch Katz was a freshman, just like Cali and me, and pretty outgoing. When he went to shake Randy's hand, I noticed a sleeve inked onto Mitch's arm. *Could these guys get any hotter?*

Starting to slur his words, making his Southern accent that much thicker, Walker leaned over to put his arm around Randy's shoulder. "What do you say we all get the heck outta here?" He had a devilish grin on his face as he winked at Cali, making both of us blush.

The rest of us agreed and made our way to the parking lot. Randy grabbed my hand once we made it out the door, leading me to his truck. "Race ya home, Walker!"

One

My college years were a blur of studying and partying. The only thing I could say held any significance was meeting Randy, the fraternity guy with the great smile. Meeting him had lifted me off the ground in an instant. And just as quickly, I'd crashed back down to earth the day I found out he hadn't held up his end of the bargain. I'd never realized "until death" would come before kids and old age for us.

I had always known that his choice to join the military would be difficult for me. When his unit was called, Randall McManus had been whisked away from me only two short months after our vows had been said. He's taken so much pride in his status as a paratrooper that I'd known he was meant for greatness. He'd held his head a little higher after he'd enlisted two days after he had graduated from college.

For what felt like forever after Randy died, I was not awake. I'd simply gone through the bare, basic motions of life. Friends and family would stop by to make sure I'd been taking care of myself from time to time. My mom did most of my grocery shopping, and she even got so fed up with my lack of cleanliness that she broke down and hired a maid. Work continued to be the only venture into normalcy I'd been able stomach. Most people stopped calling, texting, or stopping by. It's sad to say, but I was happier being left alone. I couldn't handle being bothered, constantly reminded of my 'sad situation' and being a continuing source of pity.

Walker was my most frequent visitor, pretty much like clockwork. Every Sunday at noon, I expected to see his bright green eyes light up when I opened my door. He was going through his own process of grief and loss. I think he needed the company as much as I did.

Walker Eastman had been Randy's right-hand man ever since they'd pledged their fraternity. He had even been overseas with Randy when the military-deemed accident happened. There had been some faulty cables that had snapped when the parachute tried to open. Needless to say, there'd been no condolence letter good enough from the military to cool my anger and sorrow. All of us had come hurtling down to earth that day. Walker was the only one who never said the wrong thing or pressured me into talking. I welcomed his company warmly, to my surprise. Mostly we just sat, drank coffee, and watched TV—simple yet perfect.

When I finally coaxed my eyes to open, I read eleven thirty on my alarm clock and sighed, looking at all of the pamphlets from all of the different organizations supposed to help me with my grief. I rolled my eyes and shoved them out of my mind, allowing myself to ignore them for a little bit longer. Knowing that Walker would be showing up sooner than I wanted, I fought through my down comforter to find my phone. *Maybe he won't mind missing one visit.* I really was not in the mood for cheering up that morning.

Once my phone was finally in my hand, I fumbled through my contacts, clicking on his name. Before I could even rethink the call, Walker was on the other end, declining my suggestion for a rain check. Right as I started to protest, I heard my front door slam shut. He hung up as he entered my room, his brawny arms carrying a box of donuts and coffee. I couldn't help but smile, a little relieved that Walker was just as stubborn as I was.

I felt like it was the first time I'd truly opened my eyes in weeks, and to my horror, I realized how disheveled I looked and how messy my room was. My baby blue carpet was almost entirely hidden under dirty clothes. My makeup lined up on top of the dresser was a huge mess, and I hadn't even made it out of my bed yet. I was wrapped up in the covers with all the pillows thrown on the floor. Randy had always made fun of me for being a 'pillow tosser' in my sleep. I wasn't even allowed to have beverages on my nightstand for fear of knocking them off in the middle of the night.

I cringed with shame from the mess and my wretched appearance. "Walker, I'm not even dressed. I'm sure I look like hell!" I shrieked, diving back under my blanket. I was in one of Randy's old Army shirts and basketball shorts, makeup still on from the night before and smudged all over my eyes. My dark brown hair must have looked like a lion's mane, a tangled mess. I felt it half matted to the side of my face.

I could hear Walker's deep Southern drawl through the comforter. "Come on, Mags, I've seen you at your worst. Trust me, you look like an angel compared to a few months ago."

The time Walker referred to was our darkest hours that we'd just started to break away from. The few months prior had been riddled with sleepless nights and bedridden days; we were both walking dead. During that terrible stint, we'd spent a lot of time holding on to each other for dear life, like it was the only thing keeping our world from shattering around us.

He climbed onto the foot of my king-sized bed, handed me my black coffee, and set out the food carefully. "How about breakfast in bed and a movie?" He pulled *Almost Famous* out of his jacket pocket and tossed me a smirk. The smell of the bitter coffee made my mood lift a little, and I peeked out from under my blankets.

There is no way I can turn down that smile, my favorite movie, and breakfast bribery.

"How could I say no to an offer like that?" I jumped out of my bed, tousled my hair a little, attempting to tame it slightly, and put all of the pillows back onto the bed while Walker started the movie and threw his black leather jacket onto the floor.

We climbed under the covers, cuddling down to have an awesome breakfast with good company. Walker's shoulder cradled my head as I slurped coffee from the plastic lid and let my eyes wander over his muscular, tattooed arms. I had been with him and Randy for almost every one of their ink sessions. I could imagine the swallows on Walker's chiseled chest that he gotten about a month after we met. He was handsome and tall, and he had an erotic stare that could make any girl wet within seconds. I never knew why he just jumped around from girl to girl, not even able to define monogamy. Randy had always said that being promiscuous was just in Walker's nature, and I never questioned it further.

It was comforting to have someone fill the other side of the bed. We watched the movie, reciting every line, and munched away on the glazed treats. When the credits started to roll, Walker pulled me to him tighter; he could always tell when the tears were about to start. I breathed in his mix of salty tears and men's cologne, a smell that had become a little too comforting to me recently. We lay silently while the credits played out, the movie soundtrack hushed in the background of our embrace.

When the room went silent, I buried my face into Walker's chest a little harder. "You'll never know how much it means to me that you come here every week," I choked out, unable to contain my emotions any longer. His thumb battled the tears cascading down my exposed cheek.

Walker's big green eyes were soft, a look rarely seen from the hard-ass country boy. Knowing that made his kind face and words mean so much more to me. "I'll never miss our Sunday tradition. It's the best part of my week. You still don't know how much it helps me too."

The sincerity of his words spread over Walker's face, and again, he stunned me. His chiseled jaw line, jet-black hair, and olive skin made his light eyes stand out, and when he was vulnerable to emotion, it made everything that much more handsome.

I knew our time was going to get cut short because of my father-in-law Jim's birthday party that evening. Walker had promised Liz, my mother-in-law, that he would help her with the planning and getting everything prepared, but I was not ready for Walker to pull away as quickly as he did.

Breaking our lingering stare, Walker looked over to my clock on my nightstand. "Mags, I got to head out. Liz needs me to pick the cake up for Jim's party tonight..."

As he trailed off, I watched his eyes scan over the pamphlets scattered next to my clock. Picking a few up, he turned to me with concern and frustration spreading like wildfire across his face, his green eyes darkening and his jaw flexing, burning away the loving glare I was enjoying so much. "Mags." He sighed and shook his head for a moment. "You promised."

I gaped at him, taking the pamphlets out of his hand. I looked down at a few terrible titles like, 'How to Cope with the Loss of a Spouse' and 'It's Okay to Grieve,' suddenly feeling like I was going to lose my breakfast. I took the lot of them and shoved them away in the drawer of my nightstand.

"Yeah, I know...but I just want to do this on my own. Don't worry, I set up an appointment with someone." I faked a smile, and it seemed like enough of an answer for Walker.

He stood up and stretched. "All right. As long as you're taking care of yourself, I'm happy. See you tonight?"

Trying to push away my frustration, I let my mind wander back to our relaxing morning. "Tell Liz I'll be there at eight unless she needs help with anything."

"Okay, I'll let her know." And with a quick kiss to my forehead, he was out the door. I hated watching anyone walk away from me. Being alive was hard enough, but alone, it was almost unbearable. As Walker shut my front door, I curled up in a ball on my bed and let hot tears pour again from my aching eyes.

The thought of having to spend time with a large group of people that night was almost too overwhelming. I longed to run away and hide from life for the rest of the day. It was a terrible coping mechanism I had developed, but it was effective. I cried harder when I figured there was no escape from our plans and buried my face deep into my pillow.

Randy had grown up down the street from where we'd ended up purchasing our home. He had always said that family needed to be close for when our kids were growing up. Now, silently I thanked him for forcing me into this house five minutes from the in-laws, because I needed them as a different type of support system than expected. Orlando had really turned into home for me. My heart had died there, and I was determined to revive it there eventually. It was what Randy would have wanted. He would have been so happy to know that my mom moved had here to help take care of me and that Walker had stayed, too.

"A support system is important, Mags. It doesn't always have to be you against the world, ya know."

My phone buzzed in my hand, bringing me back from my pity party and daydreams of my husband. I looked down to find a message from my mother-in-law, Liz:

Don't worry. Walker and I are taking care of everything. See you at eight.

I sighed, rubbed my eyes, and dragged myself out of bed. The clock said six, and even though I could walk to their house, I figured I needed the extra time to start putting effort into my appearance since it had been so long since I'd cared what I looked like. I made my way into the bathroom and let the water get boiling hot while I sat on the toilet, waiting.

My mind tripped back to my amazing in-laws and how important they had become to me, especially with the terrible situation we found ourselves in. Liz and Jim McManus had been more than just in-laws to me ever since Randy and I had first started dating, and I owed it to them to put on a brave face. Even though they'd lost their son, they had been so instrumental in bringing me through my grief that I worried they hadn't had the chance they deserved to grieve themselves. The shame made it difficult to even look into their eyes most of the time. It was unbearable to walk around with all the different forms of guilt inside me. I knew I had to get better for everyone's sake.

Today can be the beginning of a brand new start.

As I got into the shower, I could hear Randy's voice. "I married one hell of a woman, you know that, baby?" I smirked as I massaged shampoo into my scalp. Those are the memories I never got used to being reminded of. All of the little things he would to do to make sure I knew he loved me, that he belonged to me. I wished I had told him more how much they'd meant, how much he'd meant to me.

I miss you so much it hurts.

The hot water rushed over my pink skin while steam floated out over the curtain. I stood, holding myself, letting the water run over my body for a few moments before mustering up the courage to step onto the cold tile floor.

Without even drying myself, I tossed my hair up in one towel and then wrapped another around my dripping body. Looking in the mirror over my sink, I was disgusted at the black, puffy circles around my eyes and how hollow my cheekbones were.

Skulking back into my room, shuffling my feet along my fluffy carpet, I grabbed my makeup and turned on my flat iron. I sat cross-legged on the floor in front of the closet door mirror and began to apply eyeliner.

This had become a habit from the first time I'd slept over at Randy's room in the fraternity house. I would always take my shower first, and while I got ready, Randy would wash up. The only place for me to be able to do my primping had been on his floor, sitting Indian-style in front of a full-length mirror propped up against the wall. Randy had bought for me after I'd complained about not being able to do makeup in a fogged-up mirror.

Once my eyes were just the perfect blend of smoky gray and black, my natural curls burned into submission, I took one last look at myself in the mirror, again disgusted with my appearance. I still felt like an empty shell. It was terrible to see on my face. The lack of sleep, improper nutrition, and guilt had started to take a noticeable toll. I grabbed my blush and bronzer, blending my cheeks more to hide my uncharacteristically pale skin. One last look in the mirror, I closed my makeup kit. *This is going to have to do. Makeup can only hide so much.*

I rummaged through my closet, trying to find something to wear. All the way in the back, I found a dress that still had the tags on it from right after Randy had been deployed. I'd had a lot of free time back then, and I usually filled the void with shopping with Cali, mostly for things I had yet to wear. I yanked the dress off the hanger, slipped it over my head, and pulled on a pair of wedges. *Good enough.*

I sighed and trudged down the stairs to the freezer, taking my black-labeled savior out of his icy home. I was going to need all the help possible to put on a brave, put-together face, and whiskey was my known choice for liquid courage. *Here goes nothing.* I took one big, deep breath and headed out my front door.

SPECIAL THANKS

TO BRETT: Thank you for your big heart and even bigger personality. You helped shape this book by just being you and lending your moxie to help develop one hell of a wonderful secondary character! Love you!

TO JOSIE BORDEAUX, AUTHOR OF THE ALLURING PROMISES SERIES: I don't know if you even realize how great of a friend you have been to me or how much you influenced this book. Right when I told you the idea, I was nervous to write rom-com, not to mention erotica and you believed in me and this story! You are amazing!

TO DIESEL: (Yes, I have my dog in here, again!) Thanks for grunting, barking, growling, shoving, and stressing me out from under my desk. You have inspired one of the most enjoyable characters I have ever written, Dozer!

TO MY AMAZING EDITOR, C MARIE: My dear, you have done it again! You are simply amazing and I am so glad that we work together. Thank you for making my books blossom into so much more than I even expected them to be!

TO THE READER: Thank you for your support, encouragement and love for the written word. I love what I do and you make it possible! Don't ever forget that without readers, authors wouldn't have an audience and where's the fun in that?

NOTE FROM THE AUTHOR

Thank you for buying my novel. In doing so, you have helped fulfill a very important goal of mine. From every purchase of any of my books, I donate to the Marcie Mazzola Foundation. The mission of the foundation is to "help better the lives of abused and at-risk children; and to build community awareness regarding the needs of children."

The Marcie Mazzola Foundation was established in 2003 by my family. On July 6, 2002, Marcie died tragically in an automobile accident. Although she was only 21 at the time of her death, Marcie had experienced many things and touched many lives. She was a beautiful young woman whose inner beauty surpassed even her physical beauty because of her compassionate nature and treatment of others.

At the time of her death, Marcie was involved in a civil lawsuit against a school bus driver who had sexually abused her when she was 11 years old. Prior to her death, it had been expected that the case would be won, but since Marcie could no longer testify, it was going to be next to impossible to win. Marcie's attorney met with her family to determine if the suit should be continued. He advised the family that Marcie had confided in him her intention to donate her entire award to help sexually and physically abused children if she won the case. Once this was known, the family had no doubt that the suit had to continue.

The attorney's strong commitment to Marcie prompted him to proceed with the case, and against all odds, it was won.

Marcie's estate was awarded a monetary settlement. With her attorney's guidance and continued support, the family established a foundation as a tribute to Marcie's life, which would continue her legacy to help children.

To learn more about The Marcie Mazzola Foundation, please visit: http://www.marciemazzolafoundation.org

Marcie Mazzola Foundation
158 Burr Road, Commack, NY 11725
phone: 631-858-1855 • fax: 631-462-8544
email: info@marciemazzolafoundation.org

THE AUTHOR

Hi! I am just an average twenty-something following my dreams. I have a full time "day job" and by night I am an author. I guess you could say that writing is like my super power (I always wanted one of those). I am a lover of wine, sushi, football and the ocean; that is when I am not wrapped up in the literary world.

Please feel free to contact me to chat about my writing, books you think I'd like or just to shoot the, well you know.

Stay Connected:

KristenHopeMazzola.com

https://www.facebook.com/AuthorKristenHope

https://goodreads.com/author/show/7179522.Kristen_Hope_Mazzola

https://twitter.com/khmazz

Email: authorkristenmazzola@gmail.com